Captain Acorn

RETURNS

AVALON ROBINSON

For Iro,

When I wrote this you were just as young and small as one of the characters in this book, but someday you'll be old enough to read it for yourself. When that day comes, I hope it brings you as much joy as you bring to me.

TABLE OF CONTENTS

CHAPTER ONE
CAPTAIN ACORN EMBARKS

There was once a family that consisted of a father, a mother, four girls, three cats, and too many stuffed animals to count. Of these stuffed animals, a chosen handful was constantly crammed into a tote bag, so they could be easily hauled into the family's minivan for the sisters' entertainment. Even though they lived incredibly close to the town's center, the family often had to drive farther to get or do things they needed because the town was incredibly small. Everything from larger chain stores to movie theaters to extended family was at least an hour's drive away. So, with the exception of the three cats, who would have hated the experience and gained nothing from the destinations, the family spent a lot of time in the car together.

One particular Friday afternoon, the four sisters found themselves on a longer car ride than usual. The family was going on a weekend trip together and had already been in the car for two hours. By this point, they'd already eaten a fair amount of their snacks, listened to some of their favorite songs, and played a variety of word games that are only really fun to play once on a long car ride. Boredom seemed dangerously close to making an appearance, so they turned to a well-loved hero of theirs to save them in their hour of need.

Out from the depths of the tote bag, the youngest sister pulled out a small, brown squirrel with beady, black eyes and a frizzy, caramel tail. This was Captain Acorn, the very same squirrel who had gone on such fantastic adventures on a similar car ride and was about to go on some more.

For her part, Captain Acorn was more than ready to go on another adventure. She had already gone through the entire process of planning a new voyage, hiring a new crew (which involved another stadium full of eager, hopeful animals), and debating whether or not she should pack more cookies for the voyage. The only thing left was for Captain Acorn's beloved ship, the Golden Acorn, to finish its new paint job.

The paint job had seemed like a good idea at the time. Acorn was obsessed with keeping the Golden Acorn in tip-top condition and wouldn't stand for any imperfections. So when she had finished selecting her new crew and had gone to inspect the ship before they departed, she was incredibly disappointed to find that the rails of the ship had paint chips flaking off after an incredibly wet spring and insufferably hot summer, though her first mate, Pounce the cat, had tried to convince her that it wasn't all that noticeable, and she shouldn't worry, Acorn had been consumed by the thought of setting out to sea with her beautiful ship in a condition like that. It just goes to show that you can't unsee something you think isn't quite right, even if other people say it's hardly noticeable. So Acorn had quickly hired a paint crew of eager chipmunks (who are the best and fastest painters of the animal kingdom, if you didn't know), and set them to give the Golden Acorn a fresh coat of paint.

The problem arrived when it became clear what Acorn had just committed to as far as time is concerned. When the chief chipmunk tried to go over the paint contract with her, Acorn made him rush ahead to the final page where she signed. If she had paid a little more attention, she would have read that the whole thing would take a month, but she was so concerned with her ship's look that she didn't bother to look at that part. While she was a sharp and intelligent squirrel, when it came time to the sea, it seems that Acorn knew next to nothing about painting. In her mind, the whole thing would be done by the end of the week and then she and her crew would be off and away on a new voyage.

So it was a terrible shock for poor Captain Acorn when she checked on her ship's progress the next day and found out that she didn't have four days to wait but four weeks. The chipmunks all awkwardly tried to console her by patting her on the back with their sticky paint paws and telling her that they would work faster than they ever had for the great Captain Acorn. Acorn was too frustrated with herself to care, though, and went home to wait with paint paw prints on her back and a deflated sense of excitement.

Acorn tried her best to keep her spirits up as the wait began, but she found it very difficult when her two favorite hobbies in all the world were voyaging and planning voyages, and she was unable to do either. The crew that she'd hired were all very understanding about the delay and reassured Acorn that they would all sail with her as soon as the ship was ready, and Pounce tried to keep her spirits up by visiting every Tuesday during the wait.

Pounce was a very happy cat and was usually very good at cheering other animals up. She had never met an animal she couldn't cheer up, and it was a sort of badge of honor for her that she was so good at it. So it was very alarming for her to find out just how difficult it was to cheer up Acorn when she was this down. Nothing Pounce tried, whether it was yummy snacks or goofy voices, quite did the trick. As the weeks went on, Acorn became more and more melancholy. She stopped brushing her fur so regularly, left dirty dishes in the sink, and never strayed far from the window that had a view of the harbor. Acorn knew that Pounce meant the best, but as she saw it, there were two kinds of sadness: Sadness that can be cheered and sadness that can't, and she had the second kind.

On the fourth Tuesday, when Pounce politely knocked on the door, a very depressed voice called "Come in," from the other side.

"Good morning, Captain!" Pounce said cheerfully, "Guess what!"

I don't know if you've ever talked to someone who was as down as Acorn, but they usually don't enjoy guessing games. Acorn herself certainly wasn't in a guessing mood, and Pounce probably should have assumed that from her appearance. Acorn looked only half awake, and her tail was so messy that Pounce was a little embarrassed to see her Captain in this state. Acorn didn't look at Pounce when she came in and only stared longingly out the window towards the harbor. Pounce felt more than a little awkward in this situation. The time hadn't seemed so difficult for Pounce, who had spent the time biking to and from the harbor every day and enjoying the fresh air. It was difficult for her to imagine why Acorn was so despairing when she'd been having a rather enjoyable month.

"Look at it, Pounce," she moaned, "the ocean right there, and me! Stuck on land with no ship."

"Well, that's just it, Captain!" Pounce tried again cheerfully, "You'll be happy to know that…"

"Oh!" Acorn sighed and turned away from the window with a sweeping gesture of her paw, "I don't know, Pounce. I think the time for happiness has long since passed me by."

Pounce opened her mouth and closed it again, not really sure what to do with a statement like that, especially considering that she still had something to say that she thought would make Acorn happy. When the cat didn't say anything, Acorn sighed again and looked back at the harbor before thinking better of it.

"So, uh," Pounce said awkwardly. A lot of her excitement was being sapped by Acorn. "As I was saying, I came to tell you…"

"Oh, Pounce!" Acorn moaned dramatically. She draped herself over the couch, holding one paw to her forehead as she sighed again. "It's no use. The Golden Acorn is done for. I'll have to cancel the voyage and get a job onshore. But I don't have any talents to use on land. I did work at a pretzel stand once in high school. Maybe they'll take me back, and I can spend my days selling animals overly salted pretzels. Then they can take their salty, salty pretzels and sail away across the horizon and leave me here to waste away!"

And with those words, she flopped off the couch and lay face down on the carpet with her tail drooping out behind her. Pounce didn't really know what to do. She'd been trying her best to give her Captain some news that might cheer her up, but Acorn just didn't seem all that interested in hearing it.

"Mmm, fghmm mmmghm fffm mghh hmm!" Acorn wailed unintelligibly into the carpet, but it sounded an awful lot like: "The Golden Acorn will never be ready!"

"But that's just it!" Pounce said eagerly, leaning over the couch to address the lump of sad fur that was her Captain. "It *is* ready! I just came from the harbor, and the chipmunk crew told me that the Golden Acorn is ready!"

"IT'S WHAT?!?!" Squeaked Acorn so wildly that Pounce jumped and fell back over the couch and onto the floor where she lay in confusion, her sleek tail standing on end.

Acorn took no notice of Pounce's state of fear and leaped over the back of the couch to loom over the frightened cat.

"Is it ready? Is it really ready? Is it? Is it? Is it?" Acorn chattered so fast that the words all ran together and mostly just sounded like excited squeaking.

"Yes! It's ready!" Pounce squeaked back, but that was mostly still from fear than actual excitement herself.

Acorn started squeaking and chattering with joy as she raced around the apartment, which was very unlike her. Pounce stayed lying on the floor for a little bit longer. If you've ever been scared so badly that you fall on the floor, you'll know that it takes a minute or two to recover fully. Acorn didn't notice (or didn't care) that her first mate was lying on the ground and rushed around her home, organizing the trunks and bags that had been packed and waiting since the voyage was first delayed. Shouting excitedly about ships, the ocean, and not serving pretzels, she rushed into her bedroom, and her voice grew more distant. In the quiet, Pounce finished recovering and started to pull herself off the floor by holding onto the back of the couch.

"AND POUNCE!" Acorn almost screamed with glee, running back into the room.

WHUMP! Pounce was back on the floor in fear again.

"Pounce?" Acorn called in confusion. She looked around but couldn't see the cat anywhere and couldn't understand why Pounce wasn't running around like she was. "Pounce? Where are you? This is no time for silly hiding games!"

"Here!" Came the feeble voice behind the couch, and Pounce slowly pulled herself up again. She was definitely regretting coming to tell Acorn in person that the ship was ready and was wishing intensely that she'd sent a note instead. For her part, Acorn was too excited to wonder for more than a second why Pounce was so insistent on lying on the floor when they had a ship to get to. In another minute, Acorn had all her things stacked by the door and flung the door wide open.

"Come on, Pounce!" She called impatiently, "Get a move on! We don't have all day! The sea awaits!" And then she bolted out the door without waiting for Pounce and ran all the way to the harbor with her suitcases bumping along on their wheels behind her.

Within half an hour, the crew had all been summoned to the ship and had assembled on the deck. Acorn tried to make her usual speech about the adventure that lay before them, the trials ahead, and how much she believed in each and every one of them. It was a very moving speech that she gave before the start of every voyage, and it usually got the entire crew to stand proudly and courageously. One or two crew members would often be so overcome that they actually shed a tear.

Unfortunately, this time, most of the animals couldn't understand a word of the speech. Acorn was so excited that she talked at least three times faster than she normally did, and squirrels can talk very fast, to begin with. The crew tried their best to follow along, but it was almost impossible. Even Pounce, who knew the speech by heart, and Bunnerton, a repeat sailor, were completely lost and had no idea what was being said. When the speech was finally finished, Acorn raised one eyebrow, and all the surrounding animals realized in horror

that she had asked them all a question. There was a tense, nervous moment when no one really knew exactly what to do or say. Finally, one nervous badger cleared his throat awkwardly and gave a quiet little "Aye, Captain!"

Thinking this was as good a response as any, the other animals all followed his example and cheered in unison, "Aye, Captain!", and Acorn beamed proudly at them. They all cheered again in what Acorn took for enthusiasm, but it was actually relief at having guessed the proper response and avoided disappointing their beloved Captain before the ship had even left the harbor.

Continuing to cheer, the animals all rushed about their tasks and the Golden Acorn was soon moving steadily out of the harbor and into the vast, unknown sea beyond. And despite the long delay, all the animals had to agree that the new paint job did look wonderful.

CHAPTER TWO
CAPTAIN ACORN AND THE ORCAS

As a young squirrel, Acorn had worked very hard at her education. Her mother had pushed her to be the best student she could possibly be, and with time, Acorn became obsessed with doing well in school. It's probably why she did so well when she went away to university and why she graduated at the top of her class in the sailing program. Of course, like any university, Acorn had been required to take some foreign language courses. The sisters had tried to learn a foreign language together, and after realizing how difficult it could be, decided that if anyone could do it and do it well, it was Captain Acorn. Fortunately for Acorn, this was around the same time that a real quality program was introduced for learning to speak orca.

Now, orcas have a very complex language system that's truly extraordinary. Many animals have taken on the study of orca, but very few non-native speakers can say that they are fluent in the language. The main reason it's so complex is that it relies very heavily on making squeaking and clicking sounds. These are hard enough for some animals to make, but to make matters harder, the squeaking and clicking sounds usually have to be made at the same time. Because of this, many animals give up learning orca altogether, which is a shame because it's a widely spoken language, and it sounds very beautiful when you understand it. There's a lot of beautiful poems that are best read in orca.

Acorn didn't like the idea of shying away from a language just because it was difficult to learn. She was as fearless a student as she was a captain and threw herself into education so enthusiastically that it genuinely scared her teachers. Still, she always got good grades, so the teachers were happy in the end.

At first, Captain Acorn thought the language was incredibly easy, and she couldn't understand why so many animals found it so difficult. This was probably because squirrels are naturally very squeaky animals when they speak casually, and this lent itself very well to speaking orca. Within the first month of her language course, Acorn could squeak in orca better than all the other students and felt a sort of confidence that you can only feel while convincing yourself you're practically fluent in a language.

In the second level of orca language classes, however, the teacher introduced the click sounds. Nothing in language learning deflates your I-think-I'm-so-fluent confidence like introducing a new concept that you struggle with, and Captain Acorn certainly struggled. All at once, it felt like she couldn't get anything right, which is a truly frustrating feeling when you're trying to learn a language. She made squeaking sounds when she was supposed to make clicking sounds, her clicking sounded more like a horrible sneezing fit, and when she did manage to make the sounds at the same time, she usually ended up saying something very different from what she had originally been trying to say.

She tried everything she could think of to master the sounds, practicing in front of a mirror, repeating orca words to herself constantly, and even listened to orca audiobooks as she fell asleep at night. The teacher tried to reassure her that everyone always has some part of language learning that trips them up, but it was a little hard for Acorn to swallow since she was so used to being almost perfect at anything she did. So despite all her best efforts, Acorn always struggled a little with the clicking sounds. She still managed to pass her language class with fantastic grades, but she didn't feel that they reflected her best work.

One day early in the voyage, Acorn was in her cabin busily poring over her charts and maps. She liked to have things just so from the start of her voyage. In her mind, the best voyages were well-planned ones. It's not that she couldn't handle surprises (she actually handled them with regular ease), but having a plan helped her have a framework where surprises and unexpected adventures could happen. She had just made a note about an island she really wanted to visit when she heard Pounce's signature, enthusiastic knock at the door.

"Captain?" Pounce called through the cabin door.

"What is it, Pounce?" Acorn answered absentmindedly. She was still looking through her maps and giving a lot more attention to them than her first mate.

"There's, um, well a lot of orcas outside, and they seem like they're looking for someone in charge to talk to. We're not really sure. No one on deck knows how to speak orca." She left out that she couldn't speak orca either, but Acorn already knew that. Once, she'd tried to teach Pounce some basic orca phrases, but the only thing the cat could ever remember was how to say "This is my little brother" and "Where's the bathroom?" which are only helpful if you need to introduce your little brother to someone while you're looking for a bathroom.

For her part, Acorn was suddenly very excited and trying her best not to let it show too much, which takes a lot of self-control if you've ever tried to do it. It's not every day that you meet a pod of orcas, especially when you're the only person aboard the ship who can speak the language. She forced herself to walk up to the main deck instead of running full tilt, and if Pounce suspected anything about how excited her captain was, she didn't say anything. Then again, Pounce rarely noticed anything out of the ordinary since she was usually getting distracted and interested in anything but the situation at hand.

On deck, the crew all looked relieved to see Acorn and went back to looking eagerly over the ship's rail. Very few of them had seen an orca before, let alone a whole pod, which is exactly what was swirling around in the water next to the ship. The orcas were huge in comparison to the Golden Acorn animals, but they seemed friendly enough. Even with the language barrier between them, the whales smiled earnestly and gave little hello waves and polite nods. Ordinarily, there was still work that needed to be happening around the ship, but Acorn highly valued her crew's education and thought this was as good a moment as any to let work fall by the wayside for a little bit in favor of learning.

She joined her crew at the rail and waved to the orcas along with them. The difference was that she gave her most regal captain's wave, so the orcas would immediately know she was the one in charge.

The chief orca looked around at the others and then made a series of clicks and squeaks that meant something along the lines of, "We heard you were passing through the area, and we wanted to say hello."

Acorn smiled graciously at the orcas and cleared her throat to respond. She normally didn't feel nervous speaking to a crowd, but it's a different matter when you need to speak to a crowd in a different language from your own, and there's a whole other crowd watching you speak to the first crowd. Still, Captain Acorn was a brave and noble squirrel, and she wasn't about to let something silly like stage fright get the better of her, especially after she'd done so much to learn the language in the first place.

"Thank you," she squeaked and clicked in orca, "I'm so happy to meet you all. You have a lovely pod."

At least, that's what she meant to say. She did all right through the first half of her little speech. The problem came with the last part. In orca, a lovely pod" sounds incredibly similar to the words "try this cake." So what Acorn actually said was, "You have to try this cake." She had absolutely no idea she'd said this and let out a little sigh of relief at having successfully spoken orca.

The orcas looked at each other in complete bewilderment. They'd only wanted to say hello to a well-known sea captain who was passing through the area, and now she was offering them a cake. Orcas are very polite sea creatures and are always trying to make other animals feel comfortable and appreciated. So they all glanced back and forth at each other, wondering what to do about the situation. Acorn missed the subtle glances because she was focusing so intensely on the language, and the crew missed them because they were too busy being awed by their captain's amazing language skills.

After a long, nervous pause, the chief orca nodded kindly at Acorn and squeaked, "We would love to have some cake. We'll wait right here."

This, of course, was a complete surprise to Acorn, and her heart started pounding wildly. She tried her best to think of everything she'd read about orca customs, but nothing in any of those books had ever mentioned them asking for cake or what to do when they did ask.

"Of course," Acorn quickly squeaked, less in orca and more in fear, "just a moment please." But she had mixed up her squeaks again and had actually said, "Of course, some kelp, please."

Acorn frantically motioned for Bunnerton, the best baker on the crew, and whispered what was happening in the rabbit's ear. The poor bunny was incredibly shocked to find out that the orcas were asking for a cake and that she was their best chance for making them one. Still, she was a hardworking rabbit, who always wanted to do her best for her captain, and she dashed away to the kitchen to get to work.

Meanwhile, a large wad of kelp was suddenly tossed onto the deck by an orca, landing with a squishy thud at Acorn's feet. Looking down at the orcas, she smiled nervously at them while they all nodded, thinking that she wanted the kelp as payment for the cake she was offering. They felt a little uncomfortable (and some were even feeling irritated) that Acorn had offered cake and then asked them to pay for it, but they were all too polite to say anything. For her part, Acorn assumed the kelp must have been some sort of peace offering that the orcas were proud of, and she motioned Ethan Badgerson over.

"Please take this kelp down to my cabin and put it in a place of honor."

The badger awkwardly took the pile of kelp in his paws. He wasn't exactly sure what it had to do with anything, but he so admired his captain's ability to speak another language he didn't think to question anything, and he hurried off to the cabin with her prize.

Now came the truly awkward part of the day. While Bunnerton was furiously dashing around the kitchen covered in flour and frantically making a cake, the rest of the ship was uncomfortably still. I don't know if you've ever had a conversation in a different language than yours, but if you have, you know that you run out of things to say a lot quicker than you do in most conversations.

The crew, who didn't speak any orca in the first place, didn't feel they could just go about talking amongst themselves when the orcas wouldn't be able to understand it, so they shuffled and shifted from one paw to the other and waited in silence. The orcas felt the same way and didn't want to make the Golden Acorn crew feel uncomfortable by speaking to each other. They could have spoken to Acorn, but they were feeling so confused by the whole cake situation that none of them wanted to say anything else to this strange squirrel, who was apparently selling cake as she journeyed across the sea. So they bobbed uneasily by the side of the ship and waited, one or two of the younger orcas absentmindedly swishing their fins on the surface of the water to pass the time.

Acorn, who was feeling less and less confident with her language skills by the minute, also stayed quiet. As far as she knew, she had come this far without making any mistakes in speaking orca, and she didn't want to push her luck. She was also staying quiet because she was thinking as hard as she could about everything she'd ever read about orcas and still didn't know what the cake was all about or what she was supposed to do next. So there was a long period of silence, where no animal was speaking, and the whole situation felt more and more uncomfortable the longer it went.

Finally, Bunnerton rushed back on deck with a cake that wasn't necessarily the best she'd ever made, but admirable, I think, considering how fast she'd worked to make it. Her ears were droopy from fatigue, and her apron was covered in explosive white paw prints from getting flour on herself in her hurry. In some areas, her fur was spiked and matted where frosting had dripped and hardened. She was breathing so hard she was making little wheezing noises that made her bright pink nose scrunch and unscrunch with every breath. Acorn was momentarily worried that she might have asked too much of the loyal crew member as she watched Bunnerton exhaustedly stagger across the deck with the cake. But with a little flourish, the tired rabbit presented the cake to her captain, who gratefully accepted it. As quickly as she'd arrived, Bunnerton turned and went back below deck, where she took a good four-hour nap. It was very unlike the rabbit to leave without a word, but since it was rather extraordinary circumstances, no one felt the need to say anything about it.

After Bunnerton disappeared below deck, Acorn turned her attention back to the orcas waiting below. The orcas were all incredibly relieved that something was finally happening again and were hopeful that they might be able to leave soon. Several of them had places they needed to be, and they didn't want to be late.

"Here!" Acorn squeaked carefully in orca, "Here is the cake for you!" And for once, she actually got the sentence right.

The chief orca stretched herself high out of the water and balanced the cake Acorn was offering on her nose before lowering herself back down to where the rest of the pod could try it. Had Bunnerton stayed to watch, she would have been pleased by how much the orcas squeaked and clicked their praise of her baking, but she was already snoring softly in her bunk, and so she missed how much her cake was enjoyed.

It seemed for a moment that that would be the end of things, and both groups would go their separate ways, forever wondering why a cake had been dragged into the day's events. Acorn, however, encouraged by the success of the cake, was once again feeling confident in her language skills and tried to make small talk with the happily munching orcas.

"Do you like the cake?" She clicked while her crew leaned forward to listen as if they could understand the conversation.

"Oh, yes!" Squeaked the chief orca happily. The orcas were enjoying the cake so much that they had almost forgotten that they'd had it sprung on them. "It's delicious! Please thank the rabbit for us."

"I will," Acorn squeaked with a polite nod, "she will be very happy to know that others also think she's a great baker."

That's where Acorn went wrong again. She started to mix up her squeaks and clicks again, and the meaning of what she'd said had been changed. Instead of calling Bunnerton a great baker, she had called her a one-eyed tuna fish instead. The orcas were all taken aback by this because that was usually what they called a foolish person who wasn't looking where they were swimming, and that hardly seemed to describe the nice little rabbit who had made the cake. Up to that point, the things Acorn had said were odd, but this one completely baffled them.

"Erm," Squeaked a curious young orca from the back of the pod who couldn't take the confusion anymore, "Don't you mean baker? Or rabbit?"

"Isn't that what I said?" Acorn clicked uneasily.

Several orca heads shook to mean no.

"What did I say instead?" Acorn squeaked even more uneasily.

The orcas all grew quiet. None of them wanted to embarrass Acorn by telling her the truth, but none of them wanted to lie either. Both sets of animals fell into another long, awkward pause before the same young orca finally spoke up again.

"You called her... a tuna," he squeaked and clicked in embarrassment. "Specifically, a one-eyed tuna..."

Something about the way the young orca said it made a few other orcas cover their huge mouths, so they wouldn't laugh. It was hard work, though, and a few squeaky giggles managed to slip out. The chief orca tried to look at them sternly, but she was struggling not to giggle too. Next thing anyone knew, the orcas were all squeaking and clicking with laughter so hard that a few of them sank back below the water, and only a mass of giggly bubbles showed where they were. The crew was very confused why the orcas were suddenly laughing and looked eagerly at Acorn, thinking maybe their captain had told a really funny joke. For her part, Acorn was still processing that she had called Bunnerton a one-eyed tuna and was mentally running through everything she'd said to the orcas and understanding just how many mistakes she had made with the language.

At that moment, Captain Acorn realized one of the best things about learning a language is, it's rare for someone to be laughing at you. Most of the time, they are laughing with you, and it's actually nice for you to join in the fun. As the orcas squeaked in laughter, Acorn slowly started to squeak with laughter too. This let the rest of the crew know that it was all right to find the whole thing funny, and soon the whole ship was filled with all sorts of squeaking, tweeting, mewing, squawking, and croaking laughter. The best part of all was that everyone was suddenly on the same page because laughter is a language almost everyone understands. Sometimes, you don't even need to understand the joke to think it's funny; you just laugh because laughter with friends feels nice.

Now, at last, Acorn understood what the Orcas were trying to ask her, and the entire afternoon started to make a little more sense. This was a moment where her crew could easily see why she was such a well-respected squirrel in the world. Where this sudden turn of events might have tripped up other animals, Acorn wasn't phased for more than a moment.

She started her conversation with the orcas again, but this time, she was very careful to ask them if she had said something right or ask the right word for something if she wasn't sure. For their part, the orcas were just as polite as ever and were very encouraging as they helped Acorn through the language. Even more than before, they admired Acorn for not only being able to speak their language but being willing to take advice and correction as well. It looks good to be able to speak another language, but it looks even better to be a good student about it.

When the orcas finally left later that afternoon, everyone aboard the Golden Acorn felt that the day had been a huge success despite the mishaps. No one did ever think to tell Bunnerton that the cake hadn't actually been needed, and when she woke up from her nap, they all went to great lengths to tell her how much the orcas had enjoyed it and that she had made a big difference. Acorn herself even declared that night's dinner a celebration of Bunnerton, and each crew member went around and paid the blushing rabbit a compliment. And late that night, when Acorn finally went to bed, there was a large, squishy pile of kelp on her desk to remind her just how tricky learning another language can be.

CHAPTER THREE
ACORN'S STEALTH MISSION

While sometimes Captain Acorn could be a little self-absorbed, she was always on the lookout for ways to help animals in need. There were many animals in faraway places who could claim that Acorn had helped them when they were experiencing a crisis. There was even a colony of beavers who still sent Acorn a thank you card every year in memory of the time she had almost single-handedly saved their dams from a roaming flock of sparrows who were constantly taking them apart stick by stick and leaving behind insulting notes that were very specific and hurtful. And, of course, the Bunny Islanders still appreciated Acorn ridding their island home of a particularly bad pirate problem. So even when Acorn didn't intend to stay in a port for very long, she always left some time available just in case someone needed her help, which just goes to show why Acorn was such a respected squirrel.

When the Golden Acorn stopped for a day at Scurry Bay to resupply, Acorn went to a well-known coffee shop in town and settled herself down for a few hours just in case any animals came to find her with a problem. Pounce knew what she was doing and excused herself to spend some time playing at the beach (even though she was supposed to be overseeing the crew loading the ship). Acorn saw her playing but decided that if it helped her first mate get out some extra energy, it wasn't such a bad thing. She went back to reading her book about the history of Scurry Bay.

There was a particularly interesting part about how the mice of Scurry Bay had revolutionized the cheese packing industry, which led to the rise of Scurry

Bay's golden age. Acorn took a sip of coffee and pressed her nose deeper in her book.

"Excuse me?" A mouse asked, hesitantly approaching her table, "Are you Captain Acorn? *The* Captain Acorn?"

Acorn smiled warmly as she set down her book, and the mouse relaxed a little. "You have the right squirrel. What can I do for you?"

The mouse gulped and straightened up to make his speech. "Captain Acorn, ma'am, my uncle is the mayor here in Scurry Bay, and if you are available, he would very much like to meet with you to discuss a problem we have here in town."

He ended his speech with a little sigh and waited nervously. Acorn got the distinct impression that he had carefully memorized everything he was going to say and couldn't think of anything else unless it was part of his script. He clutched his paws nervously behind his back, and his big, rounded ears were twitching so much, it looked like he was shaking. Other animals in the shop, who could overhear the conversation, were trying their hardest to look at Acorn, without actually looking at her to see if it really was the famed sea captain. Deeply aware of this, Acorn slowly rose from the table, which gave animals at other tables more than enough time to stare at her in awe. Even after all these years, Acorn still loved the attention, and she let out a happy but still very regal sigh as she turned to the nervous mouse:

"I would be happy to meet with your uncle right away."

Acorn extended a paw to the little mouse who returned the pawshake eagerly and for a little too long. Not that it bothered Acorn. She was used to animals shaking her paw for awkward lengths of time and had mastered a way of pulling her paw back without making the other animal feel stupid. When Acorn got her paw back, she was polite enough not to wipe it on her fur, even though the young mouse's paw had been incredibly sweaty.

"Lead on, Mr...?"

Mouseton!" The young mouse stammered eagerly. He was very relieved that his speech had done so well and that he hadn't made a fool of himself in front of one of his greatest heroes. He was a simple mouse with simple goals.

With Pounce following behind (and sulking a little for not getting to play in the surf anymore), Mouseton led the way through the busy streets of Scurry Bay. Acorn was so well known in the area that many animals in the downtown district either stopped and stared at her in wonder or quickly jumped out of her way to let her pass. One or two animals gawked and pointed, which isn't very polite. Acorn was used to that kind of attention, though, and was polite enough to cover her manners and any pointing animals.

After a walk that took a little longer than Mouseton had been hoping (a group of mice asking to have their picture taken with Acorn had slowed them down significantly), they arrived at Scurry Bay City Hall. It was not a particularly impressive building in size, but that was the way mice like it. A building among mice is considered beautiful by how small you can make it and still fit your needs. Acorn actually had to duck down a little to fit through the main door. Pounce just hit her head on the doorframe.

It seemed to Acorn that Mr. Mouseton was still holding fast to his idea of not saying anything that he hadn't been able to practice for a few hours in advance. He would look back occasionally to make sure Acorn and Pounce were still behind him as he led them through the narrow hallways, but for the most part, he kept his lips pressed tightly together and looked ahead as he marched.

Finally, Mr. Mouseton stopped outside a tiny door that was beautifully carved with pictures of mice shaking hands and getting along with each other. He knocked twice, and it opened almost immediately. Mouseton stepped to the side of the door and gestured kindly for Acorn and Pounce to go through.

"Thank you very much, Mr. Mouseton," Acorn said kindly, and the little mouse looked like he might faint from the simple praise.

Inside the tiny office behind a small desk sat two very important looking mice. Acorn could tell they were important because they had incredibly long whiskers that were impeccably cared for, fancy golden wristwatches, and a plaque on the desk that said, "Mayor and Deputy Mayor: The most important mice in Scurry Bay." The oldest looking mouse leaned across the desk to shake Acorn's paw.

"Welcome, welcome!" He said in a wheezy, old mouse voice, "I am Mayor Mouseton, and this is my deputy Mousely. I hope my young nephew was polite. Please sit down. We can't thank you enough for coming."

"The pleasure's all mine," Acorn said crisply, sitting down on a chair in front of the desk and nudging Pounce to do the same. "Please, tell me how I can help your fine town."

Mayor Mouseton sighed, shook his head, and said, "We mice have worked hard to make Scurry Bay a wonderful place for all who live here and all who visit. We are proud mice, Captain Acorn. It isn't easy for us to admit when our town is anything less than excellent."

"The problem is possums. A large gang of them has been terrorizing our town every night and frightening everyone who lives here. It's gotten so bad that travelers are beginning to avoid visiting our beautiful town. These possums chase mice down the street, scatter trash everywhere, and have even painted a rather nasty cartoon of me with hurtful words like... 'Silly mouse.'"

Mayor Mouseton tried to clench his fist angrily, but he was so old and shaky it looked more like he was trying to wave to someone. It was the effort that counted, though, and Pounce and Acorn understood his bitterness.

"They are a menace," he continued, "we want our town back and will do whatever it takes to get it back."

"And you haven't attempted to engage them yourselves?" Acorn asked. She was just trying to gather all the details, but the mice looked at each other nervously at the suggestion. There are not very many animals who would willingly confront possums outright. Believe me when I say they don't take kindly to any animal telling them what they can and can't do. If confronted, possums have been known to hiss meanly in their language, which never sounds nice, and some of the meaner ones pick up animals smaller than them and dropkick them like a ball. More than a few of the bay mice had learned this the hard way and still had sore bottoms to remind them.

"It's like this," said Mousely, trying to avoid the painful memories. "They don't really take us seriously, but a well-renowned squirrel, like Captain Acorn, might just give them a good scare if you can creep up on them just right."

Acorn nodded thoughtfully, and the mice watched her eagerly. Truthfully, they had nothing to worry about. While Captain Acorn could be a little self-absorbed, she cared very deeply about her fellow animal and always wanted to help those in need. The only reason she had paused so long was that she had gotten rather lost in thought, imagining herself being a hero to the poor mice and wondering if they might build a statue in her honor or start a holiday to remember her by. It was all too easy for her to imagine a holiday with parades and fireworks and maybe even a speech by the chief mouse each year, where they would talk about her heroic deeds and how she probably had one of the most beautifully, bushy tails of any squirrel, not that Acorn was overly proud of her tail.

Acorn snapped to her senses when Pounce prodded her in the ribs with an elbow as politely as she could. Shaking her head, Acorn saw that the mice were looking around the room awkwardly and trying to pretend that they didn't notice Acorn in a somewhat trance.

"Yes!" Acorn said quickly and then a little more forcefully, so they would know she had been paying attention, "YES! A stealth mission, that is an excellent idea! I can assure you that I'll do everything in my power to ensure that I solve this problem for you. I will take the best animal I have for the job with me, and I truly believe we can sort out those possums for you."

"Oh! Thank you, Captain!" Pounce squealed gleefully, "I'm excited too!"

Acorn felt absolutely horrified and did her best not to show it on her face. Even then, she still choked on her drink and had to splutter and cough into a napkin for a few moments. It was not that she didn't believe in Pounce's desire to help, it was just that Pounce was not at all the animal she'd had in mind when she started thinking of a stealth mission.

Pounce was the second noisiest animal she had ever met. She would have been the first, but Acorn had met a parrot once who shouted everything he had to say twice, so he took first place. Even then, it was a close draw between the cat and the bird.

Pounce didn't talk loudly (most of the time), but she moved loudly. The poor cat had, in Acorn's opinion, very little control over where she placed her paws. This wasn't exactly her fault because Pounce was usually so excited that she didn't know what to do with them. It didn't help that it took very little to get Pounce excited, so she was pretty much always tripping over her own paws. When Acorn had been running through the crew in her mind, poor Pounce was probably one of the last animals that came to mind for a stealth mission of great importance.

Still, Pounce was Acorn's first mate and her best friend (though Captain Acorn only admitted that on very special occasions), and Acorn wanted to avoid hurting her feelings whenever she could.

"Yes," she said a little hoarsely, "It's very exciting. Can't wait to take you. This will all work out excellently, I'm sure."

Mayor Mouseton looked uncertainly from Pounce to Acorn like he wasn't so sure things would work out so excellently. He didn't say anything, though, since he assumed that Acorn must know what she was doing, and he didn't want to insult her prestigious reputation. Acorn always got the results, so he just assumed it must all be part of her plan. Very slowly, since he was so old and frail, Mayor Mouseton stood and made a wobbly bow to Acorn and Pounce.

"Captain Acorn, you truly are a brave and noble squirrel. We feel absolutely sure that the possums will never trouble us again if you're taking the job. The mice of Scurry Bay will forever be grateful to you and your crew."

Ordinarily, this was exactly the kind of speech Acorn loved to hear, but her mind was still spinning from the unfortunate turn of events, and she only managed to bow politely and turn to leave. As they left City Hall, Pounce talked non-stop about the stealth mission.

"Oh, Captain! This is exciting! It's been too long since the two of us got an adventure just to ourselves. I think the last time was when we had to scuba dive down to that colony of squid to give them that tentacle ointment. Remember that? Remember Captain? Because the little squids had all caught that cold, and it was wreaking havoc on that whole colony. You'd think squid would have a better immune system, but then, I don't know that many squids, so I've never been able to ask. Anyway! This is so much more exciting because this one is all about stealth! It's going to be like playing hide and seek, except if you lose, a possum is going to kick you as far as it can. But I'd like to see a possum get the best of me! If they think they can keep picking on these mice, they've got another thing coming! I'll jump right out at them and yell: AAAAAAAAAUGH!"

But what Pounce meant to be an example yell quickly turned into a real one since she wasn't looking where she was going and tripped into a trashcan, which immediately fell over and rolled down the steps of city hall with the poor cat still inside. Sighing deeply, Acorn followed after the bouncing, yelping trash can.

Later that night, as the sun set and the street lights flickered on, Acorn and Pounce prepared to make their way back into Scurry Bay. Acorn had her best sword and pistol strapped on her belt, and Pounce was carrying a boomerang. Acorn had tried to convince Pounce to bring another weapon, any other weapon, but the cat had insisted that the boomerang was an excellent choice for a stealth mission.

"Trust me, Captain!" she had said enthusiastically, "The rabbit who sold this to me promised it never fails. You have to fling it just right, but I've practiced lots, and I think I've got the hang of it now. I haven't broken anything in almost two weeks! It will be perfect for dealing with those possums! By the time they know what hit them, they won't know what hit them!"

Ordinarily, Acorn would have pointed out that what her first mate had just said didn't make even a little bit of sense, but she was feeling so stressed about the whole situation, she only tightened her sword belt nervously and shoved a tiny first aid kit into the little satchel she was planning on carrying. It never hurts to be ready.

They walked through the dark streets of Scurry Bay and met almost no one. This wasn't surprising, since, by this point, the mice were all so terrified of the possum gangs they stayed inside after dark or walked with each other in groups that were so large they were too hard to kick all at once. Acorn felt deeply angry that a set of bullies had so completely terrified a city that was otherwise charming and sweet. She turned to Pounce.

"Now," she said determinedly, "remember the plan, Pounce."

"Right!" Pounce said enthusiastically but with enough of a blank look in her beady eyes that Acorn felt it was absolutely necessary to go over the plan again.

"We're going to creep along to where the possums are seen most often. If they are facing our direction, I'll climb on the nearest roof from behind and jump down on them while you rush them from the front. If they have their backs to us, we'll creep forward until we are in striking distance and make our move. And, of course, if they find us before we find them, we pretend to be scared and frightened animals until they get close enough to show them how untrue that really is."

She had been getting more and more excited as she outlined the plan and was now rubbing her paws together in gleeful excitement. Acorn loved to teach bullies a lesson, and it had been a long time since she'd last had the opportunity. She was getting so excited, she didn't notice that Pounce hadn't really paid attention and was enjoying kicking a pebble down the dark road as they walked.

The two animals started looking carefully around street corners and peering down alleyways to keep an eye out for the possums. There was no sign of any trouble until they heard a loud crash a few streets over and mean, nasally voices laughing. Acorn signaled to Pounce to follow behind silently and hoped that the cat would be able to manage it as they crept down a dark alleyway towards the noise.

Acorn was actually impressed with how well Pounce was doing. The alleyway was crowded with metal trashcans and empty boxes, any of which would have made a tremendous amount of noise if they tripped, which Pounce was often more than ready to do. The cat was nimbly navigating the maze, though, and Acorn felt a little swell of pride as she watched her first mate jump lightly over a box, shimmy around an overturned trashcan, and complete a very complex cartwheel to get past some loose garbage. It wasn't that these acts in themselves were impressive (especially since Acorn had just done them similarly, using a frontpawspring), it was that Pounce of all animals was doing them. Acorn made a mental note as she did a backbend over another downed trash can to tell Pounce how proud she was when they got back to the ship.

As they made their way through the alley, the voices grew louder, and now they could hear the nasty comments the possums were making.

"You see how far I kicked that mousey yesterday? He won't be able to sit for a week!"

"Silly mouses! Thinken' they can get past us!"

"Mouses are a joke! This our town now!"

There were other, much more unkind things the possums said that I don't feel like repeating. Acorn and Pounce had already heard more than enough to convince them that these possums were the worst kind and were giving a bad name to possums everywhere. Possums can be lovely, hospitable animals and are very protective of children. Some of the best daycares in the world are run by possums.

Peering around the corner, Pounce and Acorn could see a gang of possums huddled together in a deserted street, snickering with each other. They weren't far away at all, but they had their backs to Acorn and her first mate, so they hadn't seen them yet.

"Don't worry, Captain," Pounce whispered deviously, "I've got this."

Acorn felt sure Pounce had never had anything less in her life and desperately wanted to know what her first mate was planning to do. Before she could say anything, though, Pounce had whipped out her boomerang and hurled it at the possums. Acorn clapped her paws over her mouth to keep herself from gasping and only just managed it. It was a testament to her self-control that she didn't outright yelp in horror as the two animals watched the boomerang slice through the air.

The possums had no idea what was coming for them, and for a moment, it looked like Pounce might have actually done something incredibly clever, which would have been a first. Acorn valued Pounce greatly, but cleverness wasn't one of the first strengths she would have listed about the cat. At the last second, though, the possums all bent down to look at something on the ground, and the boomerang zipped neatly over their heads, missing them entirely. Still slicing through the air, it curved around a nearby shed and disappeared from view. There was a long moment of dumbfounded silence, where Pounce didn't seem to fully understand what had gone wrong, and Acorn didn't know exactly what to feel. In the space of about three seconds, she had gone from horrified to intrigued and finally landed on disappointed, which is quite the emotional rollercoaster to go on in a very short amount of time. The possums were still there, though, and needed to be dealt with.

"Right," Acorn whispered to Pounce, who was still looking expectantly at the point the boomerang had disappeared from, "Good, erhm, work Pounce. So now I'm going to creep around to…"

But Acorn didn't get to finish explaining her plan because there was a quiet whooshing noise rapidly getting closer to them. Acorn had just enough time to dive roll out of the way and hide behind a barrel (you don't get an international reputation from having poor reflexes), but Pounce was nowhere near as quick.

The boomerang had come back to Pounce sure enough, but from behind. It smacked the unsuspecting cat in the back of her head and sent her sprawling forward, where she landed against a barrel, tipped into it, and let out a little yowl of terror and surprise, which is very understanding considering the circumstances.

The unfortunate fact about one thing going wrong in a plan is that it usually unravels the rest until there isn't really any plan left to work with. In an instant, Acorn could see that their plan to surprise the possums from behind was done for. The possums, who'd all looked up at the noise, quickly swarmed around the barrel and fished out the poor unfortunate cat.

It was bad enough that Pounce had been hit in the head with a boomerang and fallen in a barrel, but to make matters worse, it seemed the barrel had been a sort of local trashcan for particularly nasty garbage. The cat that the possums pulled out by the tail was covered head to toe in slimy bits of fish, fruit peels, rotten vegetables, and one or two painfully sticky candy wrappers. To cap off the look, Pounce had a Seagulls Cereal box stuck on her head, which just added further insult to injury since that was far and away her least favorite cereal.

"Wot's this?" Said the biggest possum, who was holding Pounce by the tail and seemed to be in charge of all the others. "What're yous doing?"

Possums gangs, while large and intimidating, aren't known for trying particularly hard in school, and this gang leader was one of the worst. Despite the danger of the situation, Acorn cringed inwardly at his grammar and wondered if there was any kind of tutoring program offered in Scurry Bay.

From inside the cereal box, Pounce gave a defiant cry of "Fighhrm merg fers ter fers!" The possums didn't understand a word of this, but Acorn did. She'd gotten into enough pillow fights with Pounce to let off steam over the years to recognize the muffled cry of "Fight me face to face!"

With the cereal box still stuck on her head, the head possum lifted Pounce high and drop kicked her painfully in the rear. Pounce let out a muffled cry of surprise and pain. She wasn't as small as the mice they were used to drop kicking, so the possum was only able to aim Pounce into another trash can across the street, but it was still painful and humiliating for the cat. The possums all roared with laughter, and a few more were almost wheezing and had to sit down on the street to catch their breath.

Acorn's fur prickled with sheer fury, but she wasn't staying hidden pointlessly. She was biding her time. It wasn't easy for her. Acorn was a fiercely loyal squirrel, and it enraged her to see Pounce being treated so horribly. All she wanted to do was teach the possums a lesson. She was a clever squirrel, and she knew that it wouldn't do Pounce any good to burst out into full view and get drop kicked.

At last, the possums' laughter subsided, and they all moved to fish Pounce out of the trashcan. As they went, they all turned their backs to Captain Acorn, who seized her opportunity immediately. Cinching up her sword belt, Acorn darted forward and quickly scaled the nearest streetlamp. The possums were grasping around the bottom of the trashcan for Pounce, who sounded like she still had her head very much stuck in the cereal box.

"You there!" Acorn shouted furiously from the top of the street light. Every single possum turned to look at her, and when they did, they formed a neat little line. This was, of course, exactly what Acorn was hoping they'd do. With her shrillest battle cry, Acorn managed to swing herself completely around the top of the lamp post once and then shot away feet first toward the possums. Every single possum was so shocked at the sight of a furious squirrel hurtling towards them that none of them thought to move. As a result, Acorn hit the first possum full in the chest, and the force carried her and the possum through the rest of the gang. All the possums toppled like bowling pins, and the animals ended up in an undignified pile. All except for Acorn, of course, who landed nimbly in front of the pile, and Pounce, who was still in the trashcan and struggling furiously to get her head out of the cereal box.

Acorn drew her sword and glared down at the possums, who all looked equal parts shocked and terrified, and said, "Not so tough now, eh possums? Only strong when you can pick on animals more helpless than you?"

She raised her other paw and gave a loud whistle through her large two front teeth. The local mouse police came running, looking shocked that Acorn had overcome the gang so quickly. While they rounded up the possums, Acorn hurried over to the trashcan to help Pounce out, who had just pulled the cereal box off her head with a triumphant "Aha!"

"Are you all right, Pounce?" Acorn asked briskly. She could see that for herself and was deeply relieved that the cat hadn't been hurt, but it still seemed polite to ask.

"Oh, yes!" Pounce said a little too hurriedly, and Acorn helped her climb out of the trashcan. "I'm fine, Captain! Just fine!"

"Lucky yor baws was here ter save yeh," the possum leader grumbled at Pounce, who tried to look brave and ferocious, but her ears drooped nonetheless.

"I'll thank you not to speak to my first mate that way," Acorn hissed as the Scurry Bay police department pawcuffed the possums. When the possums only hissed and spat meanly, Acorn swelled in size, and her fur spiked with anger. Still, she tried to stay calm as she spoke. "You know, I feel truly sorry for you. I have had the pleasure of meeting many wonderful possums in my voyages, and you are here disgracing their good name. You have the power to be kind and considerate but would rather be rude and harsh. You could be strong and help others, but you choose to be mean and pick on anyone smaller than you. You act big and tough, but really, you're just scared. Deep down, you're not angry with me; you're angry with yourselves. And I feel sorry for you because you don't have to be those bad things. No one's forcing you to do them. You can choose to be better."

And with a regal swish of her tail, she turned to help Pounce pull sticky garbage out of her fur as the possums were led away.

Acorn quickly wrapped up her business with the mice, shaking paws, nodding humbly to all their thanks, and graciously refusing any kinds of gifts or payments. Pounce said nothing and spent the time trying to rub the fish smell off herself and peel away some of the candy wrappers that were still stuck fast. By the time the mice disappeared with the grumbling possums, Pounce had managed to tidy herself up a bit, but she was still rubbing the sore spot where she'd been kicked.

It was a very sad, droopy tailed cat that started walking back to the Golden Acorn with her captain. Acorn felt almost as miserable, watching Pounce walk. She cared deeply for the cat and greatly cherished her happy personality, so it was strange and saddening to see Pounce feeling so down. Acorn felt nervous and uncomfortable, which were very rare things for Acorn to feel. She wanted to cheer Pounce up, but since that was usually what Pounce did for her, she wasn't really sure where to start. It's very difficult to be lighthearted and encouraging when you're used to being stoic and brave, but Acorn still felt she owed it to Pounce to try.

"Well!" She said briskly, "We sure taught those possums a lesson."

"Huuuuuuuhm." Pounce moaned in agreement.

"I don't think they'll be a problem for Scurry Bay anytime soon. That's another legendary adventure for our reputations, isn't it?" Acorn continued, trying not to show how uncertain she was feeling.

"Huuuuuuhm." Pounce sighed in a way that seemed to mean, "If you say so, Captain."

"And you know," Captain Acorn said, getting a sudden idea in her desperation, "I don't think I ever could have had an idea as good as that."

"As good as what?" Pounce said in a glum voice that told Acorn she was only asking to be polite and wasn't actually curious.

"Your diversion!" Acorn blustered theatrically, "It was brilliant! If you hadn't fallen into that mess, they would have seen me coming, and everything would have been ruined!"

Pounce's ears perked up a little bit, and she stole a glance at her captain. Pleased that her plan was working, Acorn went on thoughtfully. "You know, I don't know that I can think of a more selfless thing for an animal to do. To jump into the middle of all that just to give her captain the chance to get all the glory in the stealth mission, what character! It takes a real cat to do something so selfless and clever."

Acorn's first mate picked up her tail and stood straight and tall as they kept walking.

"Do you really think so, Captain?" she asked hopefully.

"I really do," Captain Acorn said warmly, giving the cat a caring pat on the back. And then, because it seemed like a more special occasion that needed it, added, "My dear friend."

From then on, whenever Pounce told the story of the stealth mission, she talked about her part in it with so much pride that other animals started to see it in the same light and admired her a little more for it. If she heard her first mate telling the story, Acorn would just smile and shake her head. The telling grew with time, but more than anything, she just felt relieved to have Pounce back to her happy, loud self.

Chapter Four
Captain Acorn Explores Music

By this point in the car ride, the sisters were startled by their parents turning up the volume on a particularly upbeat song, which made them wonder why Acorn didn't have more of an interest in music. Acorn wondered that herself, and about a week after they sailed away from Scurry Bay, she decided to do something about it. Captain Acorn had never really given much thought to how hard it might be to learn a musical instrument, so she quickly came to the conclusion that it couldn't be that difficult, and there was no time like the present to start. Sitting in her cabin one night, she started filling out an order form.

The trouble started when the Golden Acorn made a mail stop at a small island port. Pounce, who always took care of hauling the mail up so Acorn could wave to all her fans down below, noticed a large box addressed to her captain. This alone wasn't enough to raise any suspicion since Acorn frequently got gifts, but the sender's name on the package definitely worried the cat. It was from somewhere called Loud Lemmings Music Shop, and it was a heavy box. As Pounce sorted the mail, she wondered what her captain could possibly want from a music shop.

As it turned out, the cat didn't have to wait very long to find out. The next afternoon, just as all the crew was finishing up their biggest chores and starting to think about taking a nap, a horribly loud squawking sound blasted throughout the ship. Many animals on the crew thought it was a bird in distress and started running around, looking for who to help. The birds on the crew, who knew what a bird in distress really sounded like, almost looked more alarmed since they had absolutely no idea what the sound might actually be. A few animals were so frightened of the noise (that kept squawking without stopping), they yelped in terror and ran around in fear. One or two unfortunate animals ran straight into each other, and Bunnerton wound up flat on the deck with a badly skinned paw.

In no time at all, the crew was yelling and wailing much louder than the squawking noise, and Captain Acorn burst out of her cabin to investigate the whole thing. The moment she was on deck, the animals immediately fell silent. There's nothing like someone walking towards you who seems completely un-bothered by something you're scared of to make you reconsider if it's actually all that scary in the first place. Acorn was looking particularly fierce, and she marched down the deck with one paw on her hip and the other holding some-thing the crew couldn't recognize. The animals all shuffled from one paw to the other, feeling embarrassed by how they'd all reacted to the sound. It was then that they also noticed the squawking sound had stopped, and they felt even more embarrassed since none of them were sure how long ago it had stopped and if they had all been screaming about nothing.

"What," said Acorn calmly when she was standing in front of all the sheepish animals, "in the name of all walnuts, are you all screaming about, may I ask?"

No one said anything. None of the animals wanted to be the one to admit out loud to their captain that they had been running and screaming because they'd heard a scary noise. Acorn wasn't about to let it go that easily, though, and raised her eyebrows severely and started tapping her paw on the deck while she swished her tail back and forth with impatience.

Finally, Bunnerton, still holding her sore paw tenderly, stepped forward and cleared her throat with a quiet little cough. "We, um… We heard a… a scary noise, Captain."

Captain Acorn pinched the bridge of her nose with a paw and sighed. "You heard... a scary noise, and you all panicked?"

The crew all nodded and muttered things that sounded like, "Yes, Captain" and "that pretty much sums it up." Acorn sighed again and squeezed her eyes shut for just a moment.

"Well," she said at last, "I can't pretend that I'm not disappointed that you all reacted so poorly to the possibility of danger, but we all make mistakes. In the future, please try to remember your training and not panic because of... scary noises. Any questions?"

A young otter named Maisy Slickfur raised her paw politely, and Acorn nodded regally for her to speak.

"Excuse me, Captain Acorn, ma'am, but do you know what the sound was?"

"I didn't hear it," Acorn said loftily, "Please describe it to me."

Slickfur looked a little uncertain at her other crewmates, but she cleared her throat nonetheless and made her best impression of the squawking noise, which was actually surprisingly good, and the other animals were genuinely impressed and nodded approvingly.

Acorn suddenly understood exactly what Slickfur was describing, and she felt a little flustered herself. She'd been unpacking her instrument from the music store and had given it a little test, even though she hadn't practiced at all yet. It hadn't been the best sound, but that hardly seemed like a good reason for her whole crew to panic.

"Why!" She blustered, "It was only this!"

And she held up the object in her other paw. What was meant to be a grand moment of reveal fell flat since none of the animals on the Golden Acorn recognized the instrument. Slickfur raised her paw again.

"Yes, Miss Slickfur?" Acorn sniffed impatiently.

"Excuse me, Captain... But what are those?"

"They're bagpipes, of course!" Acorn said a little irritably, which is understandable, considering how much her crew had been panicking while she was practicing. The crew made a collective "Oh" noise, which Acorn took as appreciation, but they meant with slight fear. None of them had heard bagpipes played up close before, but if it made squawking noises all the time, they felt certain they weren't going to enjoy them.

This, of course, is a little unfair to bagpipes. They really are a beautiful instrument and can stir your heart or even make you cry in the right circumstances. The trick is playing them right, and very few have a good grasp on exactly what that trick is.

As confident as ever, Acorn didn't think it would be all that difficult to learn to play the bagpipes not only correctly but excellently. She marched back down to her cabin with her tail still swishing back and forth and within a minute, the squawking sound of the bagpipes had started up again. The crew was ready for it this time, but knowing what the sound was didn't make it any less annoying or horrible to hear, much to their disappointment.

Over the next week, the crew came to hate the sound of bagpipes. Acorn was a dedicated student in anything she tried, and music was no exception. She firmly believed that if she was going to get better at her new instrument, she needed to practice them as often as possible. She wasn't wrong. For years, people have tried to find shortcuts in learning a musical instrument, only to find that practice is the best way. The unfortunate thing about Acorn's plan was how often the crew heard her practicing.

There are two big problems with playing bagpipes on a ship. The first is that bagpipes are one of the loudest instruments you can imagine. If you've never heard bagpipes played up close, imagine standing in front of a large moose who's singing opera in a very high pitched voice, and you'll have some idea of what I mean. The second problem is a ship has only so many places you can go to get away from the sound. It's all fine and good if you like the sound of bagpipes, but most people like them best when they are played well. In the case of the Golden Acorn, the bagpipes were not being played well.

Much like with the orca language, Acorn had met her match in something she was trying to learn. She had watched the instructional videos that had come with the instrument at least half a dozen times and had read an entire book on bagpipes cover to cover, but they still sounded like Pounce trying to sing when she had a cold, which was not pretty at all. It was quickly getting harder and harder for Acorn not to get frustrated, which is never a good thing when learning something new. It's not that Acorn only liked things as long as they were easy to do, but she liked to see progress, no matter how small it was, and so far, she couldn't see any progress. She was a determined squirrel, though, and she refused to quit, practicing every moment she had a chance around her work (because, of course, she would never under any circumstances neglect her duties as captain).

The sound of the bagpipes, which had been so terrifying to the crew when they first heard them, was now just completely annoying to listen to. It wore on and on, and while they deeply admired their captain's dedication to practicing, it was particularly difficult to listen to a beginner try to improve. Still, no one dared say anything and tried to find any way they could to distract themselves from the noise.

It was not an easy task. As I've said, there are very few places you can go on a ship to hide from something like bagpipes. It took no time at all for the crew to find out just how true this was. The Golden Acorn was an impressively large ship, but it wasn't so big that it could hide the crew from bagpipe practice. Animals started spending their free time in the kitchen and pantry, convincing themselves that it was a little quieter there. A few animals, Pounce included, started trying to "out noisy" the bagpipes by loudly singing whatever song popped into their heads. Unfortunately, this only made the noise on the ship worse, and after a few arguments between the crew (one of which I'm sorry to say ended in a scuffle), the singing animals tried to find new ways to ignore Acorn's music practice.

Some of the more dramatic crew members took pillows from their bunks and tied them around their heads with extra bits of rope. Of course, this looked absolutely ridiculous to the rest of the crew, and they couldn't help making one or two jokes about it. The animals with pillows on their heads had their hearing muffled only enough to not hear the jokes but still hear far too much bagpipe practice.

After two weeks of almost non-stop bagpipes, the crew finally broke.

"I can't take it anymore!" wailed Slickfur, burying her face in her paws a little dramatically. "It's inside my head, and it won't stop!"

Beaverov gave the distraught otter a comforting pat on the back and turned to Pounce, who was clutching her paws and looking around at everyone with worried eyes.

"She's right," the beaver said, "it's just too much. Maybe the captain doesn't know how well the sound carries over the ship."

He looked uncomfortable just suggesting that Captain Acorn might not be completely knowledgeable about something on the ship. It was an odd moment, where all the animals wanted to agree with Beaverov and while not wanting to say anything at the same time. Most of them just settled for staring at the deck and shifting from foot to foot.

What no one had mentioned was that Acorn's playing had actually improved slightly over the last three days. She was finally able to carry more than three notes, and she didn't make half as many warbling and croaking noises as she had on the first day. No one had mentioned it because they had all been so consumed by the sound that they were well beyond noticing any difference in Acorn's playing. They had no idea that Acorn was barely able to tell the difference herself anymore, but being a determined squirrel, she was trying her best to push through the difficult learning process and was practicing more than ever.

For a good fifteen minutes, the entire crew of the Golden Acorn stood on the deck, not making eye contact with each other and feeling more uncomfortable with the situation by the minute. The only sound to be heard was the crash of the ocean against the ship and the never-ending warbling of the bagpipes.

As it turned out, Pounce was the first one to do something and took more responsibility than she ever had before. Pounce had many wonderful qualities, but an ability to take charge wasn't one of them, which is one reason why she and Acorn worked so well together. Acorn absolutely loved to be in charge, and Pounce couldn't think of anything she liked less. The little cat dreaded the idea of taking command far more than she dreaded the idea of talking to Acorn about the bagpipes. Still, she had seen her captain face her own fears on countless occasions, and she figured now was as good a time as any to follow Acorn's example and face one of her own. If you ever see someone stepping completely outside of what they're usually comfortable with, you know things are truly serious.

"All right, All right," she snapped, clutching her paws harder than ever. "Let's go talk to her. *All* of us."

While everyone much preferred the idea of Pounce going to talk to Captain Acorn without them, they saw that it wasn't fair for her to go alone, and they all nodded their heads in agreement and moved towards the captain's cabin. Pounce knocked on the door and then knocked again louder to be heard over the noise of the bagpipes.

"Come in!" Captain Acorn called happily in between bursts of bagpipe music.

The crew all shuffled into the cabin, which proved to be a little difficult. Acorn had made sure that the captain's cabin was the largest on the ship, but she also had a large crew. If she'd known that every single animal on her crew had been on the other side of her door, she would have never invited them all in, but there they all were. Acorn was too surprised by the whole thing to say anything, and the crew was still too embarrassed to consider how tight the room might get.

By the time the entire crew had fit in the cabin, several smaller animals had almost suffocated between the bigger ones, and the bigger ones were trying their best not to move an inch or breathe too deeply. The crowding of the crew into Acorn's cabin was followed by one of the most awkward pauses to ever occur at sea. No one said anything, and a few dozen pairs of eyes searched for anywhere to look but at each other. For her part, Acorn had recovered from her surprise and was patiently waiting for someone to say exactly why they all felt the need to come to talk to her. No one did, though, and the pause stretched on to a record uncomfortable length.

The reason the pause was going on for so long was that Pounce, who everyone was waiting on to speak up, was one of the animals nearly suffocating in the crowd. When they had all filed into the cabin, she'd been suddenly caught in between Badgerson and a very large frog named Ribbetstein. Squished between them, she was having a very hard time trying to get free, and the two larger animals had nowhere to move to help her out. They weren't enjoying having a cat stuck between them any more than Pounce was enjoying being the one stuck, and the three animals were all wiggling uncomfortably and making grumpy noises. The more time went on with no one saying anything, the more desperately Pounce wanted to get free. She was now feeling the full weight of taking responsibility and was sure that she had already messed the whole thing up.

Fortunately for her, while badgers have soft, grippy fur, frogs are typically much more slick and slippery. So when Pounce had managed to wiggle just far enough to one side, Ribbetstein gave her a hefty shove, and she slipped around his slick middle and shot from between the two animals to freedom. In fact, she launched so quickly she rammed into a few other unsuspecting animals like Bunnerton, who was kind enough not to make much of a fuss and helped the breathless cat to her feet, giving her an encouraging pat on the back. The lucky thing for Pounce was she'd been launched toward the front of the crowd and was now standing (a little worse for wear maybe) right in front of Captain Acorn's desk, where she could resume taking responsibility.

With Pounce now front and center, Acorn felt like they might actually get to some sort of explanation, and she felt relaxed enough to set her bagpipes down on her desk and start polishing them.

"Good afternoon, Pounce," she said contentedly, "To what do I owe the pleasure of having my entire crew in my cabin?"

Pounce tried her hardest to say something, but instead, all she did was open and shut her mouth a few times and grip her paws tighter than ever. If Acorn had been looking at her first mate instead of polishing her instrument, she might very well have been very concerned for the cat. Acorn was very fond of Pounce and had challenged animals to a duel more than once for insulting her first mate without Pounce ever knowing. She deeply cared if the cat was happy or not. So if she'd been looking at Pounce instead of her bagpipes, she probably would have turned all her attention to making Pounce feel at ease until she could say what was on her mind. As it was, Acorn was looking intently at what she was doing and couldn't see Pounce's discomfort.

"Go on, Pounce," Acorn encouraged her, "Say what's on your mind."

"Slight… Slight problem on the ship…" Pounce finally managed to gasp, and the heads of the other crew members all bobbed up and down in silent support of her statement.

"With what?" Acorn asked, not really concerned if it was only a slight problem and not a terrible problem.

"M-music."

All the heads bobbed again. Everyone thought Pounce was doing terrifically, given the circumstances.

"Ah, yes," Acorn said absentmindedly, "Music."

A few heads dropped in defeat. Acorn was not entirely grasping the point. She was a clever squirrel when she was paying attention, but all her focus was directed to her bagpipes at the moment.

"It's just..." Pounce tried again nervously while several crew members nudged her eagerly from behind, "Well, you see... it's just... well, it's a little... much..."

"What is?" Acorn said briskly, hardly looking up from polishing her instrument

"The bagpipes, Captain." Pounce squeaked so nervously, she almost sounded like a set of bagpipes herself.

Captain Acorn stopped polishing and looked intensely at all her crew but at Pounce particularly.

"The bagpipes?"

"Yes, Captain," Pounce was almost wheezing from nerves. She had never been this responsible or forward for as long as this, and the experience was stressing her out beyond all belief. "The bagpipes." And all at once, understanding dawned on Acorn's face.

I think they would have been able to manage if Acorn had gotten extremely angry and yelled that she could do whatever she pleased and shook her paw at the crew. They would have been scared out of their wits, but they would have managed to take it. Acorn just wasn't that kind of squirrel, though. She had been raised to treat her fellow animals kindly, no matter how disappointed or upset she was, and it wasn't in her nature to yell at others because she was frustrated. Instead, Acorn started to fidget uncomfortably behind her desk, which only made the crew feel more uncomfortable, so they started fidgeting more. In the long awkward pause that followed, the cabin was full of squirming animals, who wouldn't make eye contact with each other. The only sound was an occasional cough that made the whole room feel even more awkward.

Finally, Captain Acorn cleared her throat and spoke. "So what you're saying is that I'm bad at playing the bagpipes?"

Instantly, the room was full of surprised and reassuring animal noises.

"No! No! That's not it at all, Captain!"

"You're coming along really well!"

"Never heard better bagpipes from a beginner!"

The animals certainly weren't lying. In fact, they truly believed that Captain Acorn must be improving (even if they didn't know enough about bagpipes to tell for sure) because they had always seen her succeed at anything she tried her paw at. But sometimes, you can be so eager to reassure someone that they stop believing you're genuine, which is rather unfortunate all around because nothing gets accomplished, and you only end up moving backward.

"It's just," Pounce's voice cracked her throat was so dry from nerves, "It's just... how much bagpipes, Captain."

"How much?"

Pounce tried to say yes, but she had reached the limit of her bravery and could only make a strangled squawking noise that sounded surprisingly close to bagpipes. Since Acorn was now looking directly at Pounce, it was very clear to her how stressed her first mate was.

Acorn was a very compassionate squirrel, and she had an amazing ability to appreciate when an animal was challenging themselves to do better. It didn't matter to her if they didn't quite do whatever they were trying perfectly, it only mattered to her that they were doing their best. So while Pounce was making her nervous squawking noises, Acorn appreciated her first mate's courage.

The rest of the crew shuffled uncomfortably in the crowded office, but Acorn surprised them by smiling warmly at the nervous cat.

"It's a bit crowded in my cabin at the moment," she said finally, looking around at the crew, "I'm glad you all came to see me, but I think we could all use a little more space. So if you would all kindly go back on deck, Pounce and I will discuss the bagpipes issue and let you know what we decide."

Every animal in the crowded cabin let out a huge sigh of relief, and Pounce stopped making her squawking noises and smiled at Acorn, if not a little shakily.

As usual, Acorn had found a way out of their problem, and the crew all felt their hearts swell with pride to be sailing under the leadership of such a compassionate and caring squirrel. With the exception of Pounce, the crew all jostled and squeezed against each other in an effort to make their way to the door.

"And I hope," Acorn said with a kind smile as the crew moved out of the crowded cabin, "that in the future, you always feel you can come to talk with me about a concern. It might just save us more time in the future. Although, maybe come just one at a time?"

And as the crew left Acorn and Pounce and went about their usual chores, they couldn't help but agree with their captain.

Even if she was a particular and strong-willed squirrel, Acorn wasn't an unreasonable one. In the end, she and her crew struck a deal that left everyone feeling they could tolerate the situation. For the rest of the voyage, every Tuesday afternoon at three, it officially became music hour. The bagpipes would start up, and the crew would stuff in earplugs, cover their ears with their paws, or volunteer to go up in the lookout, which was usually an unpopular job.

In time, and with far more practice than even she had expected, Acorn was actually able to play a few songs correctly and nicely enough that the crew didn't mind her playing them outside of practicing hours. Acorn took to sitting in the lookout at sunset and playing a song or two before she stared intently over the sea, which she always thought added a flare of drama to her image. Not that it needed much more.

Chapter Five
Pounce Almost Ruins Everything

The adventures of Captain Acorn were paused very briefly when the parents pulled the car into a drive-through coffee shop, so the mother could get something to drink. The girls knew to stay quiet when their father was ordering because it's hard enough to hear what the cashier is saying through that microphone, let alone with an entire adventure aboard the Golden Acorn happening in the background. So they waited patiently for the break in their story to be over.

While they waited, the oldest sister remembered that in an earlier adventure aboard the Golden Acorn, there had been talk of getting an espresso machine. The whole incident had started when Pounce had misunderstood something that Acorn had been trying to tell her and thought Acorn was going to install an espresso machine on the ship. As it turned out, they had actually gotten a massive treasure from the ocean floor, which was nice as well. Pounce had never really stopped wishing for an espresso machine, though. So the sisters all agreed after their mom got her coffee that it was high time Pounce got her espresso.

Acorn herself had never really forgotten how badly Pounce had wanted an espresso machine. Pounce thought she had, but Acorn couldn't quite ignore how excited Pounce had been when she thought they were getting the machine. It was something that had actually kept her awake on a few nights, pacing around in her cabin.

On the one hand, Acorn was incredibly fond of her first mate and was deeply grateful for her friendship all these years. Acorn prided herself on being a good friend. In Acorn's mind, there were a lot of different ways to be a good friend to someone, but one of the best ways was gifts. Not gifts like meaningless things that were the wrong color, didn't fit or didn't interest the animal in question in the first place. Gift-giving in Acorn's world was an art form. If anyone received a gift from Captain Acorn, it was likely something that they had mentioned in passing a long time ago, but wanted very badly. Once in college, Acorn's roommate had mentioned that she liked Russian dolls on her way out the door. When her birthday came, Acorn gave her at least ten different sets of Russian dolls that were all hand-painted and personalized. Acorn took gift-giving very seriously.

So, on the other hand, knowing that Pounce had been wanting an espresso machine was a torturous thought for Acorn because that was probably the last gift an active cat like Pounce needed, but it was still something that the cat wanted badly. The problem with cats (or at least, one of their problems) is that they are absolutely terrible about limits when it comes time to food and drink. Pounce was even worse than most. Acorn forever had to remind her about the risk of tummy aches or sugar crashes, and Pounce was forever forgetting that the warnings had been given. More than a few times, Pounce had been forced to report to Acorn with a terrible stomach ache and spend the rest of the day in bed, which left both her and Acorn in bad moods. The squirrel had wondered more than once in fear: if sugar could cause so much trouble, what could caffeine possibly do?

So very wisely, Acorn had always looked for ways to keep Pounce away from caffeine. Most of the time, it was relatively easy for her to keep the cat from trying it. All Acorn had to do was usually point out some other tasty treat, and Pounce would be so happy she would never even know that she was being distracted. For Acorn's part, the occasional sugar rush seemed like a small price to pay to avoid the unknown of caffeine.

Acorn very likely could have gone without ever giving in if Pounce had whined and complained about not having the espresso machine. Unfortunately for the squirrel, her first mate had an incredibly good attitude about it and didn't pester her about getting one. This was the worst thing that could have happened for Acorn because it made her feel like Pounce deserved it as a treat.

One day, after a particularly bad bit of going back and forth on getting one, Captain Acorn finally decided to buy an espresso machine. The next day, when they pulled into a port to pick up supplies and drop off some mail, Acorn disappeared in town while her crew worked on loading the ship. No one minded since they all assumed she had important captain things to do that likely would benefit them all, and they weren't entirely wrong about that.

Just as the crew loaded the last of the food supplies and were all eagerly staring at the new candy load, Acorn reappeared with two shop rats, carrying a large crate behind her. The crew said nothing as Acorn showed the rats where she wanted the crate in the kitchen and tipped them generously, thanking them for all their help. The rats nodded respectfully and hurried away, obviously very eager to tell anyone who would listen to them about how they had helped the famous Captain Acorn with a bit of shopping

If the crew thought Acorn would tell them what was in the crate right away, they were disappointed. Acorn hummed to herself and circled the crate with her paws clasped behind her back. She could never turn down the chance for a dramatic reveal, and showing the crew that she'd bought them an espresso machine was one of the best opportunities she'd had in a long time, and she was loving every minute of it.

It wasn't until Pounce squeezed through all the crew to get a good look at the crate that Acorn finally decided it was time for the big reveal. Twirling a crowbar in her paws, she wandered over to one side of the crate and set to work opening it. In a matter of seconds, the planks had fallen away, and the crew all gasped at the huge, sparkling espresso machine that lay inside.

"Ta-da!" Acorn said with her paws proudly on her hips. It was hardly necessary for her to say it since just seeing the espresso machine was surprising enough for the crew. Still, she wanted to say it, and she was the captain and could do what she wanted. In response, the crew all gasped and made all sorts of delighted noises.

"Captain! It's beautiful!

"Is this the newest model? I knew you only got the best for your ship!"

"Captain! You spoil us! You really do!"

The animals of the Golden Acorn all crowded around the espresso machine, but none more so than Pounce, who actually pressed her face against it and hugged it while she squealed with delight. In an instant, the cat had dashed off for mugs and spent the rest of the night learning how the machine worked and making coffee for her crewmates. Acorn watched from a distance and tried her best to feel happy for the somewhat jittery animals, but she couldn't shake the feeling that something was going to go terribly wrong on the ship before all was said and done.

As usual, Acorn's instincts proved to be accurate. You don't become a world-class sea captain from having poor instincts, I can tell you that much. In this particular case, though, Captain Acorn very much wished she would be wrong and was more than a little disappointed when she wasn't. The first day after getting the espresso machine, Pounce had already learned so much about coffee making, she'd had four cups before the rest of the crew had even finished their morning chores and was the most hyper Acorn had ever seen her, which is saying a lot.

This wouldn't have been a problem if Pounce had lots of work to do, but as it was, she managed to finish all of her chores in under thirty minutes and wasn't exactly using her time well when she was done. By the time Acorn had finished studying their course and had left her cabin for breakfast, the entire ship was already rowdy, which is not at all how Acorn liked to keep her ship. This was mostly because Pounce was standing on the biggest table in the kitchen, a bandana tied around her head, reenacting the Golden Acorn's famous battle against the nasty Captain Hamsterton, much to the laughter of the entire distracted crew.

"Hem, hem," Acorn said from the doorway with her arms folded across her chest disapprovingly and her foot tapping on the floor, which is much more intimidating from a squirrel because they have bigger paws to tap with.

Immediately, the entire crew jumped in surprise and scrambled around to look busy and get back to work. All except for Pounce, who didn't notice the change taking place in her audience and attempted to recreate a particularly intense part of the battle by leaping from one table to the next. Unfortunately, for whatever energy caffeine had given Pounce, it hadn't made her anymore graceful, and she landed awkwardly on a stick of butter on the next table, slipped, and faceplanted into the bowl of scrambled eggs, which flew in all directions and coated the entire kitchen.

Besides being disappointed by the loss of the scrambled eggs, which was one of her favorite breakfast dishes, Acorn was deeply annoyed to have her ship in disarray and to be covered in breakfast food herself. She stopped tapping her foot and strolled in front of Pounce, who had finally noticed her annoyed captain and was looking about as guilty as a cat covered in scrambled eggs can look.

"Pounce," Acorn said calmly, less because she actually felt calm and more because she was trying to be. "While I appreciate your enthusiasm for recreating one of our greatest victories, it is not one of your responsibilities on my ship, and it's not yet free time."

Pounce wilted a little and looked intently at her paws. The motion dislodged some more eggs from behind her ears, and they slipped onto the floor with an awkward plop. She saluted Acorn apologetically and rushed off to find something more productive to do. As she ran off, though, Acorn noticed that her tail was swishing spastically from side to side, and her eyes were still wide and twitching uncontrollably.

The second day wasn't much better. Pounce, now so consumed by coffee, it was hard to imagine what she had been like before, had eight cups before breakfast was even finished and broke the ship-wide record for the fastest time completing all her chores. This would have been a good thing if she hadn't decided that she would make up more chores for herself to fill all her extra time. The ones she came up with were all good in theory but terrible when performed, and Acorn found herself devoting her day to rushing around the ship and undoing Pounce's well-meaning disasters.

First, the hyper little cat decided to make the bed of every single crew member on the ship. Acorn had once told her about a cruise she had taken with her parents, where the beds were made every day, and the staff left a little chocolate on the pillow. Pounce did her best to do the same for her crewmates, but with less success. For starters, they didn't have any individually wrapped chocolates, so Pounce put a handful of chocolate chips on everyone's pillows. This would have been fine except that they had been sailing through tropical waters for the last week, and the heat was more than a little intense. The chocolate chips quickly melted on every single pillow, and Acorn was left reassuring distraught animals that it was only chocolate on their pillowcase and would come out in the laundry.

The other problem with the bed making was how fast Pounce worked. She'd learned to make beds from Captain Acorn, which was a flawlessly perfect method the squirrel had developed over many years, so there was nothing wrong with how the beds were made. The problem was more with who was still in the bed. Pounce worked so quickly, she completely missed the fact that Beaverov was still in bed with a head cold, and the unsuspecting beaver was suffocatingly tucked under the sheets before he knew what was happening and couldn't get free. By the time Acorn figured out where the muffled cries for help were coming from, the poor Beaverov could hardly breathe. Acorn saw fit to bring him some hot tea personally and give him an extra day off to recover.

In the afternoon, Pounce found a new disastrous, made up chore to spend her time. If Acorn saw anything of scientific interest on her voyages, she very often took a sample of it to bring back to the Squirrel Observatory for Science and Discovery back in Old Harbor, even though she had never really forgiven them for only naming a park bench after her in her honor. Pounce knew this about Acorn since she very often went with her captain to collect the sample, and decided it had been too long since any science had happened aboard the Golden Acorn.

Acorn had just come on deck from checking on the chocolate-stained laundry when she noticed Pounce dangling from a rope tied around her back paws and soaked through and through in seawater. Badgerson was holding the other end of the rope and looking very unsure of himself. Acorn sighed and wondered why she had ever thought her beloved ship could handle an espresso machine.

"What is the meaning of this?" She tried to ask her question calmly, but the more coffee Pounce drank, the harder it was for Acorn to be calm and patient.

"Ah! Captain!" Pounce said in an excited voice that was half laughing and half yelling. She only talked faster as she went on until all her words started to blend together into one gigantic, excited slur. "I spotted some very interesting science things off the side of the ship! Badgerson here has been lowering me down, so I can try to collectasample! I'm very excited! I think this discovery could be huge!"

The hyper cat set to checking the knots on her rope with shaky, excited paws, and Acorn took the chance to turn to Badgerson.

"What exactly did she see?"

"It was, um… It was a piece of seaweed, Captain Acorn, ma'am…"

All at once, Pounce dove off the edge of the ship and Badgerson had to brace himself to keep a good grip of the rope in his paws. He looked sheepishly over at Captain Acorn, who was sighing again and holding a paw to her forehead.

"Would you like me to pull her back up, Captain?"

Acorn slid her paw off her face and tried to maintain a look of authority.

"No, no," she said finally and gave Badgerson a little pat on the shoulder. "Let her have her fun. Maybe it will tire her out."

I hate to admit it, but it was a wildly optimistic hope. Badgerson and Acorn both knew it deep down, but the badger still gave a very respectful nod to his captain as Acorn sighed again and walked away. She spent the rest of the afternoon trying her hardest to undo the mess she had created with the espresso machine and getting nowhere.

The final straw came on the third day. Acorn was busy at work in her cabin, studying charts, planning ports to stop in, and writing a new song to play on the bagpipes that she thought would make a good jig. She was tapping her paw happily and humming to herself when there was a knock at the door.

"Come in!" She called in a sing-songy voice as she made another note on the music sheet. The door creaked open, and Maisy Slickfur slipped into the cabin. She made a crisp little salute and stood at attention, but the corners of her mouth were twitching.

"Captain, I have a situation to report."

Acorn looked up sharply from her desk and the pen she'd been absent-mindedly gnawing on with her buck teeth as she thought fell out of her mouth. It wasn't that she didn't know how to handle a situation, whatever it might be, but more that there had been far too many situations in the last three days, and she was getting tired of them.

"Another?" She sighed and closed the notebook. It's hard enough to write music, but a situation that needs your attention makes it impossible.

"It's Pounce, Captain Acorn, ma'am," Slickfur announced.

"What has she done now, Miss Slickfur?"

"She's... well... She's stuck in a trash bag. It's making a sort of crinkly noise whenever she moves, and she seems to think that it's chasing her. She's running around the deck, and she's too fast for any of us to catch her and get the bag back off her."

Slickfur was a very professional otter and managed not to laugh as she said this. Even though it was the funniest thing that she'd seen since her great-uncle Rupert had once accidentally tripped and fallen face-first into a bowl of raspberry salmon jello. Acorn pinched the bridge of her nose with her paw and groaned.

"Pounce…"

The corners of Slickfur's mouth twitched again. She was getting dangerously close to laughing out loud. Acorn was observant enough to see that and while she could see how the situation could be viewed as funny, she was not in the mood for laughing herself.

"Thank you, Miss Slickfur," Acorn said curtly. "You may go. Please do your best to stay out of her way. I will be there in just a moment."

Acorn was very good at not taking her frustration out on the wrong people, so while Slickfur could see how irritated her Captain was, she knew it wasn't directed at her, and she rushed out of the cabin to go find a place where she could laugh about the whole thing.

For her part, Acorn was deeply regretting buying the espresso machine. She felt very irritated with Pounce for causing so much chaos on the Golden Acorn, but more than that, she felt irritated with herself for allowing it all to happen. Still, she was a responsible squirrel, and she knew how to step up when she needed to.

By the time Acorn reached the deck, Pounce was still racing around in the trash bag. What Slickfur had failed to mention was that Pounce was also yelling at the top of her lungs. Most of it was impossible to make out, but every now and then, she passed near enough to Acorn for her to understand some of it to be yells like "I'M TRAPPED!" and "THIS IS HOW IT ENDS!" Pounce had always reacted to things a little larger than life, but in this instance, the caffeine from the espresso was making it a thousand times worse.

Acorn would have found the whole thing just as funny as Slickfur did if it wasn't for the fact that Pounce had already managed to smash a couple of barrels to matchsticks in her panic and run into several unsuspecting crew members, who were now rubbing sore knees and elbows or looking around in confusion for what had hit them. While it was very tempting for Acorn to feel irritated and frustrated with her first mate, she realized that she simply didn't have time to do that since Pounce was on the verge of smashing a lifeboat and a couple more crew members.

Taking a deep breath, Acorn raced across to the mast, careful to step over Beaverov, who was rubbing a large, painful-looking lump on his head and looking confused. In a flash, she had a sturdy rope tied around the mast and was racing back to the ship's rail with the other end clutched in her paws.

"Stand back!" She yelled to the surrounding crew, and they all ran away to a safe distance, except for Beaverov, who sort of crawled while still holding his head.

Acorn lowered the rope to the deck but still kept a firm paw grip on it and waited. Pounce was on the other side of the ship, but she was quickly heading back in Acorn's direction, still yelling wildly. She zoomed straight towards where Captain Acorn was waiting.

"I'm trapped! I'm trapped! I'm HNNG!" Pounce made that sound because she had just run full speed into the rope that Acorn had pulled tight at the last second. The cat had been moving so fast, she actually folded over the rope with all four paws off the ground, and Acorn had to brace herself to keep her footing. With a tremendous thump, Pounce landed on the deck in a heap, and Acorn quickly leaped forward and freed the frantic cat from the trash bag.

Of course, once Pounce didn't have the trash bag on her head anymore, she saw how ridiculous she'd been. Nothing brings you down from being hyper quite like extreme embarrassment, and Pounce was very embarrassed as she looked up at her irritated Captain. Pounce didn't really know exactly what to

do with all this embarrassment, so she tried acting like there was nothing to be embarrassed about, which is actually a pretty common response.

"Oh h-h-h-hey, C-c-c-captain!" Pounce stammered from where she was squished on the deck. She was so hyper from all the coffee, she couldn't even speak normally. "W-w-w-what's up-p-p-p? D-d-d-did you n-n-n-need s-s-s-something?"

It's genuinely incredible that Acorn was able to keep control of her frustration, but as I've said before, you don't become a world-famous sea captain by losing your temper when your first mate is making a fool of herself. I will say she did heave the biggest sigh she'd ever heaved in her entire life, but it had been a very stressful couple of days.

"Bunnerton? Badgerson?" Acorn called from where she was still sitting on her twitching, hyper first mate. The two crew members (who happened to be two of the only animals who hadn't been injured in the rampage) came forward a little nervously while still keeping a safe distance from the spastic little cat. "Will the two of you please escort Pounce downstairs to her bed and make sure she stays there for the rest of the day?"

Badgerson and Bunnerton looked like they would rather do anything else, but Acorn had saved the Golden Acorn from a coffee-related disaster, so it seemed like the least they could do. Pounce was rather unceremoniously carried below deck, twitching and stuttering the whole way. Acorn spent the rest of the day cleaning scraped knees and fetching ice packs for unfortunate animals who'd had their heads bonked during the trash bag incident.

In the end, Captain Acorn had the best solution, even if Pounce didn't enjoy it very much herself. That night, she called Bunnerton to her cabin for tea.

"How long does it take a single animal to clean all the bathrooms on the ship?" Acorn asked as she poured the happy little rabbit a steaming cup of tea (It was a great honor to have tea one on one with Captain Acorn). Bunnerton was in charge of organizing the chore chart on the ship and knew it inside and out. She proudly rattled off her answer at lightning speed.

"About two hours, Captain."

"And how many bathrooms do we have?" Acorn took a thoughtful sip of tea.

"Six bathrooms, Captain."

"Excellent," Captain Acorn clapped her paws together and rubbed them mischievously, "Bunnerton, I'd like you to adjust the chore chart accordingly. I believe Pounce has more than enough energy to do that chore by herself, don't you?"

Bunnerton wasn't quite as skilled as Slickfur at holding in laughter, and she clapped a paw over her mouth to hide a giggle. Acorn didn't mind a bit, though, since she always enjoyed someone appreciating how clever she was. In fact, with a less than dignified snort, she started laughing herself, and soon, the cabin was filled with the delighted snickering of the two animals.

"Yes, Captain," Bunnerton finally said between giggles. "I think she does."

Pounce did indeed have enough energy to do the whole chore by herself, but she didn't enjoy a minute of it. The day after she finished solo cleaning every bathroom on the ship, Pounce was back to her normal self. Well, maybe not entirely normal. Acorn saw her repeatedly grab her head with both paws on several occasions when she thought no one was looking and knew her first mate was nursing a wicked headache from her caffeine crash. Unsurprisingly, Pounce didn't drink any coffee for a few days.

Captain Acorn was a kind squirrel, and she kept the espresso machine on the ship because she didn't want to punish all the other animals who hadn't done anything crazy or destructive. But from then on, it was very simple to keep Pounce from drinking too much coffee. On mornings when Pounce had more than one cup, all Acorn had to do was make a passing comment about the chore chart, and she knew Pounce wouldn't even dream of having a third cup of coffee.

Chapter Six
The Crew Has a Night Off

It was always important to Captain Acorn that her crew worked as hard and as well as they were able. She expected a lot of them at all times because she was used to being the best in the world and didn't like the idea of ever being anything less than that. They practiced their jobs constantly and to perfection. Anything other than their best effort was unacceptable when sailing aboard the Golden Acorn, and every animal knew that. Animals didn't flock to the crew auditions because they thought they were going on a pleasure cruise. This was the big leagues, and, for the most part, every single animal who was ever hired to sail with Captain Acorn gave their best effort at all times because they knew that if they could make it on her crew, they could make it anywhere.

Still, for her high expectations, Acorn always wanted to make sure that her crew was well taken care of. That meant that she gave the entire crew a night off when they were at a particularly fun location at least once or twice during her voyages. She would arrange for a trusted friend at the port to come watch the ship for her and then assemble the entire crew on deck before she let them loose. Even though she was giving them a night off, she usually told her crew her expectations for their behavior to make sure no one did anything that could embarrass her.

The crew had all been talking for weeks about where they might get their night off. Pounce, who was never quite able to maintain a lofty distance of authority like Captain Acorn, had excitedly told the crew that their last voyage had stopped off at a port, well-known for being a city built almost entirely out of bounce houses. Of course, this far exceeded the wildest hopes of all the crew when they imagined the fun they might have, and they spiraled into a near frenzy of anticipation.

One day, when the Golden Acorn pulled into another port, Acorn called the entire crew to attention for an announcement. At this point, they had been getting so excited about their night off that none of them could really hold still. Pounce's tail was swishing spastically back and forth, even though she hadn't had a drop of coffee in three days. Slickfur was wringing her paws round and round without end. One particularly eager hamster was dancing from paw to paw until Badgerson laid a heavy paw on his head to force him to stop jumping up and down. Even then, Badgerson himself was rocking back and forth on his heels in excitement.

"Animals of the Golden Acorn!" Acorn began with a grin. She was deeply enjoying how eager all the animals were. "As you know, I like to give each of my crews at least one night off during the voyage, just to give them a bit of fun. I'm very happy to tell you that tonight is your night! Would any of you like to know what I've arranged for you?"

It was a slightly ridiculous question to ask. Every animal on deck was almost shaking from how badly they very obviously wanted to know. Acorn only asked because she loved a good dramatic reveal, and the best way to have one is to build up a lot of excitement nice and slowly. The animals all nodded their heads in unison so vigorously that a few of them stumbled and almost fell over.

"I'm particularly excited about this outing." Acorn smiled, "We are here the same weekend as the island county fair! What do you think of that?"

The animals all let a series of "ooh"s and excited gasps that told Acorn they found the idea of going to the fair a very exciting thing.

"Yes!" Acorn cried, feeding off their excitement, "And that's not the best part!"

Every set of eyes on the crew widened in shock. They had all thought it was amazing enough that they would be going to a fair, and none of them could imagine what could be better than that.

"I have a good friend here," Acorn continued with a cheeky grin, "and he's very kindly arranged tickets for all of you for the rides and carnival games. So I expect all of you to have a fun evening and enjoy yourselves on your night off. That's an order."

All the animals of the Golden Acorn were more than ready to take that order seriously, and they all dashed off to their bunks and hammocks to get ready for the fair. Acorn watched them all go with a smile, feeling very pleased with herself that they were all so excited. She made a mental note to thank her friend for the fair tickets when she saw him next.

An hour later, the crew of the Golden Acorn disembarked and nearly ran into town in their hurry to get to the fair. They all had fistfuls of tickets clutched in their paws and wings, and everyone had a different plan for what they wanted to spend their precious tickets on. The evening air was full of excited chatter.

"I hope I can win one of those giant stuffed bears!"

"I want to go on every ride twice!"

"Do you think they'll have funnel cake? It's been so long since I've had funnel cake!"

"I looked up ways to actually win the ring toss. I don't care how many tickets it takes, I'm going to win!"

Over the course of the next hour, almost all of those wishes came true. Beaverov had, in fact, won at the ring toss and was still boasting to anyone who would listen. Hamsterly was trailing behind the rest of the crew under the weight of a teddy bear three times his size. Slickfur and Pounce were sharing a plate of funnel cake that was entirely too big for both of them, and Badgerson was still leaning in the bushes, trying not to be sick, after going on a spinning ride twice in a row. They were all pausing by Badgerson to decide where they wanted to go next when they found something incredibly surprising.

"Is that- is that the captain??" Bunnerton asked incredulously, pointing her paw discreetly through the crowd.

Every single crew member in earshot spun around to look where Bunnerton was pointing. Sure enough, there was their captain, wearing her nicest scarf and walking into the fanciest restaurant in town across the street from the fair. That wasn't what surprised them, though. Captain Acorn had a flair for the fancy and often dined at fancy places when they went ashore. What surprised them was who she was with.

There was a tall, handsome squirrel none of them had ever seen before, sweeping off his top hat and gesturing Acorn through the door he was holding open for her. Bunnerton and a few other crew members blushed at how handsome he was, and a few even started giggling. Others made grumbling sounds that meant something along the lines of, "He's not *that* handsome!"

Pounce, who knew Captain Acorn better than anyone else and thought her captain always confided in her, was more shocked than anyone and stood with her mouth hanging wide open. Actually, Acorn had told her just that morning that she was going out to dinner, but Pounce had been too busy pretending she had coins for eyes to pay any attention and had, as usual, missed what Acorn was telling her. So Acorn had decided that was a free pass at keeping it extra secretive and hadn't repeated herself.

From where they were standing, the crew could just see Acorn smile warmly and laugh as she walked into the restaurant with the handsome squirrel. The crew stood still in shock, and no one knew what to make of what they just saw. If they were going to make it to the glass bottom boat tour, they needed to get moving, but the idea of Captain Acorn going out to dinner with a handsome stranger was just as interesting of an adventure. After a moment of thought, the crew all nodded to each other silently and did their best to sneak up on the restaurant.

It wasn't easy going. None of them were particularly sneaky animals, and it's much harder to be sneaky when you are excited. Several crew members bumped into each other, trying to sneak in the same direction, and Bunnerton tripped rather dramatically over Slickfur when she tried to tiptoe forward while the otter was choosing to crawl low to the ground. Animals passing by in the surrounding area kept looking over at the Golden Acorn crew in confusion as they very obviously crept up to the restaurant. Fortunately for them, Acorn and her mysterious companion had their back to the crew as they went in; otherwise, they would have been noticed in an instant, and all their fun would have been over before it could even begin.

Once outside the restaurant, the crew all made a complex series of paw gestures at each other that they meant to be signals to hide but just confused each other instead. After finally understanding the motions (which included a brief and silent argument), they all concealed themselves behind sandwich board signs, bushes, or directly under the large front window of the restaurant. Peeking around corners and through leaves, they all did their best to watch their captain and her mysterious companion.

Inside the restaurant, Captain Acorn was greatly enjoying herself, mostly because of the company she was in. If she had known her crew was just outside watching her, I think she would have been humiliated. Fortunately for everyone, Acorn's crew was better at hiding behind streetlamps and bushes than she would have imagined, and she had no idea they were watching her every move. As the squirrel with Acorn pulled out a chair for her and then sat down himself, she settled in happily for what she hoped would be a pleasant evening.

The squirrel with her was none other than Edward Squirrelson; someone Acorn had known before she was a captain and hadn't seen since. They'd gone to school together but had both gone their separate ways after graduation to establish their sailing careers. Squirrelson had been a talented captain but had quickly found that he had much more of a knack for management and had started his own shipping company that specialized in importing and shipping sea salted acorns. The business had been going very well, and he now had a small fleet of ships that reported to him.

"It's fantastic to see you again, Acorn," he said warmly and spread his napkin across his lap. Both of them tucked into the complimentary walnut bowl the waiter had just set in front of them. "I hope this voyage has been just as exceptional as all your others."

"Quite!" Acorn said, a mouthful of walnuts tucked into her cheeks. In squirrel culture, it's actually polite to talk with your cheeks full. It lets another squirrel know that communication with them is your first priority. It's important that the food is tucked into your cheeks, though, or the whole gesture falls apart. "From what I hear, your shipping business is putting all the rest to shame. I always knew you were destined for greatness."

"I could say the same of you," Squirrelson said kindly. They both raised their glasses and toasted each other.

While the two squirrels were thoroughly enjoying their time together, the things they talked about weren't all that interesting. They spent a good deal of time discussing the Golden Acorn, Squirrelson's shipping business, and even the weather. The only thing they said that could be remotely interesting to anyone else was when they reminisced about a certain time at school when one of them had ended up on the roof of the library with a bright red flag in their paws and leading the students below in a rousing song to celebrate the end of the semester.

"Ah," Acorn sighed fondly, "what foolish young squirrels we were. Thank you again for the fair tickets. I'm sure my crew is having the time of their lives."

Acorn was absolutely right. Her crew was having the time of their lives, but for a vastly different reason than she had originally planned. Back outside the restaurant, the crew was getting more and more curious. At first, it was fun to watch their captain so intensely through the windows, but there's only so much fun you can get out of watching two squirrels talk to each other when you can't hear what's going on.

"What are they saying?" Slickfur hissed impatiently, while Pounce shushed her loudly. Not because shushing Slickfur did anything to improve how much they could all hear, but because Pounce was trying her hardest to think, and she couldn't do that and answer questions at the same time.

"We need better ears!" She exclaimed at last. All eyes turned to Bunnerton, whose face drooped in annoyance when she realized what they were expecting.

"No, thank you!" Bunnerton said curtly, and she reached up to stroke her long ears protectively. "My ears are *not* for casual eavesdropping."

When her fellow crewmates only stared at her expectantly, she got a little more flustered.

"Besides!" Bunnerton insisted, "They're not perfect! My ears need to be pointing in just the right way to pick up something that far away, and I get so tired if I have to hold them like that."

The crew all exchanged glances before Pounce and Slickfure crept over to Bunnerton, and each took an ear. Bunnerton sighed in protest one more time just so everyone knew she wasn't particularly happy with her job in all this spying; nevertheless, she started directing Pounce and Slickfur. The other animals were dying with curiosity, but they tried to stay quiet to let Bunnerton and the others work.

"Move my right ear a little to the left... No left!... Your other left!... Stop it Pounce! You won't make my ears work any better pulling on them like that... That's it! That's it!... Oh, wait, no. That's just the family having dinner on the other side of the restaurant..."

After a few more minutes of maneuvering the poor unfortunate rabbit's ears and arguing amongst themselves, Bunnerton suddenly stopped them with an excited squeak: "Wait! That's it! Stop right there! I can hear them!"

Every animal leaned in eagerly, briefly forgetting that it was only Bunnerton who would be able to hear anything. Bunnerton's face was screwed up in concentration as she listened to the conversation inside, and Slickfur and Pounce tried their best to hold her ears in the exact same position. Once or twice, a couple of younger crew members opened their mouths to interrupt, but they were quickly silenced by a harsh glare from Pounce, who didn't spend all that time positioning Bunnerton's ears just to have her not catch anything.

"They're talking about the weather…" Bunnerton said at last, still scrunching her nose with concentration. All the animals around her sighed grumpily since the weather wasn't exactly the most interesting thing they could have heard.

"Wait! Now they're talking about how good it is to see each other again…"

The crew all perked up again and leaned in closer.

"…She's saying it's been too long since they last did this… He says she's right…"

The crew was now leaning in around Bunnerton's ears, as though they might catch bits and pieces of what she was hearing.

"He's saying she looks lovely… That it's the perfect evening for… Yes! It's a date! They're on a date!"

"I knew it!" shouted a young weasel, gleefully jumping up and down. The noise and movement caught the eye of just about every patron in the restaurant, and the crew had only just enough time to flatten themselves on the sidewalk below the windows before Captain Acorn turned around to see what all the commotion was about. Not seeing anything outside, Acorn shrugged and turned back to her date.

Outside on the sidewalk, Beaverov used his very large tail to flatten the noisy weasel on the ground and keep him quiet. The crew slowly crept back to the edge of the window, nervously peeking into the restaurant to make sure the coast was clear. Bunnerton, who'd been pulled to the ground by her ears when

Pounce and Slickfur dove out of sight, was rubbing her head in pain and casting deeply judgemental looks at her fellow crew members.

No one took much notice of how annoyed Bunnerton was, and all whispered excitedly amongst themselves about their discovery and how clever they had been in finding out. Of course, none of this would have been necessary if Pounce had just paid attention when Acorn had told her about the date, but none of the crew realized that (Pounce included), and they continued congratulating themselves for a job well done.

They were so proud of themselves, they didn't notice Acorn and Squirrelson dabbing the corners of their mouths with napkins and rising to leave. They might have never noticed if Bunnerton, who was still a little too annoyed with her fellow crew members to be celebrating, hadn't looked through the window and saw the pair walking to the door. The alarm was raised, and all the animals of the Golden Acorn rushed to hide behind anything available. By the time Acorn and Squirrelson stepped outside the restaurant, there was no evidence of the crew, except one or two paws that dashed back into view to pull an exposed tail into hiding.

Acorn and her companion strolled away down the sidewalk, blissfully unaware of how closely they were being watched. As they walked away, the crew slowly emerged from their hiding places and exchanged thoughtful glances. It was a moment of decision, and they all made various gestures and signals about whether or not they should follow their captain. In the end, curiosity got the best of even the most unsure animal, and they all resumed their ridiculous "sneaking" walk, as painfully obvious as it still was. It all goes to show how powerful curiosity is and how hard it is to resist.

It wasn't easy going for the crew. Acorn and Squirrelson were still talking of shipping, sailing, and old memories, but they were looking around and admiring the various shops and sights in town as well. Once or twice, the crew had to dodge wildly and hide behind anything available, whether it was a lamppost, box, or passing animal (who were not at all pleased with being used for a hiding place).

It shouldn't be counted against Captain Acorn that she didn't notice her crew following her. She was an incredibly observant squirrel but not around the clock. If this had been a dangerous mission or adventure, all of her squirrel senses would have been on high alert, and she would have known if a moth was flying too close to her. This was a night off, though, and she was letting herself relax and not worry since (she thought) her crew were all safely hidden away at the fair where they would never see her, let alone dare to spy on her. So she walked along, blissfully unaware that her entire crew was creeping along behind her.

By the time Acorn and Squirrelson stopped again, they were in a local park that was largely abandoned but lit nicely with hanging lanterns. The crew were incredibly relieved to be somewhere with more readily available hiding places since it's fairly difficult to walk, hide, and spy all at the same time. As Acorn and Squirrelson looked around the park and chatted happily, the crew stuffed themselves into nearby bushes and trees. They were getting rather good at hiding by this point and felt proud of themselves.

"What a lovely park!" Acorn mused happily, "It reminds me of the park on campus where they would have those Tuesday night dances. Do you remember?"

"Ah yes, said Squirrelson, "How could I forget! We were the tango champions, after all!"

The two squirrels looked at each other, grinned, and then started stretching and jogging in place to warm up. The crew all felt very confused but got their answer a moment later when Squirrelson and Acorn started a tango so fantastic every animal hidden from sight felt absolutely breathless.

It was suddenly very easy to see why Acorn and Squirrelson had been tango champions at school. If you've ever tried it yourself, then you know a tango done right looks stunning, and a tango done wrong looks like two people arguing about how to land a plane. Acorn and Squirrelson were getting the tango very right. Any animal watching them would have guessed that they had been practicing for weeks instead of dancing on the spur of the moment after not seeing each other for years. They even managed to pull off a particularly complicated move that involved Squirrelson throwing Acorn in the air and Acorn landing on one foot and immediately doing a complete turn. They ended the whole dance with a very complicated dip, where Squirrelson could have easily smashed Acorn's nose on the pavement if he did it wrong (which is why you should always dance with someone you trust not to drop you), and both squirrels grinned at each other.

If you've ever watched a truly spectacular performance, you know there's a sort of excitement that comes with it and makes it so you can't help bursting out in applause when it's over. Acorn's dance with Squirrelson was no exception. The unfortunate thing about that is that if you're trying to spy on someone and stay out of sight, the last thing you should do is burst out clapping. The crew couldn't help themselves, though, and they all broke into applause and cheers for their talented captain without thinking.

It only took them a moment to realize what a huge mistake that had been, and they immediately fell silent again, but it was too late. Captain Acorn spun around and glared into the darkness, and Mr. Squirrelson looked incredibly confused. The crew members all looked at each other in horror from their various hiding places, wondering if there was any possible chance that Acorn would think another group of animals had done the cheering. Of course, there was no chance of them being so lucky, and Acorn called out in a very crisp, short voice:

"Would the crew of the Golden Acorn come forward *immediately*."

The animals of the Golden Acorn all stepped forward with slow, mournful pawsteps, as if Acorn had just ordered each and every one of them to walk the plank.

Almost every single animal present felt like she had, and the ones who didn't were the animals who were too angry with their fellow crew members for clapping, even though they had cheered right alongside them.

When they were all standing in front of her, shifting uneasily from paw to paw, Acorn started staring each and every one of them down with a hard, disappointed gaze. Most animals can keep a gaze like that up for a few seconds, but Acorn was not like most animals. Even after a full minute had gone by, Acorn was still staring down her crew, who was getting more and more sheepish and ashamed by the second.

"One. Night." Acorn finally said curtly, and her tail was twitching with irritation. "I give you one night off, and this is how you spend it? Spying on your captain? Your *captain*?" she repeated incredulously, and the crew all started to see what they'd done from Captain Acorn's perspective.

Every animal hung their head in shame. There was a horrible, long, pause when everyone on the crew tried not to make eye contact with Acorn, who was still glaring at them in turns while her tail twitched back and forth. Squirrelson, though he hadn't done anything wrong, was looking the most uncomfortable. It's incredibly awkward to be caught in the middle of a group being disciplined that has nothing to do with you, but you can't exactly leave either. He tried to pass the uncomfortable time by looking up at the twinkling lamps like they were the most interesting thing he'd ever seen, but even that didn't really help much. He started shifting from one leg to the other and clasping his paws behind his back just to unclasp them again and scratch at his ears.

The only animal who wasn't feeling uncomfortable was Captain Acorn herself. It wasn't the first time she'd caught one of her crews doing something they shouldn't have, although this one was making her feel particularly annoyed, especially since she was now replaying the whole tango in her mind and hoping that it had matched up to her performance standards. She was a very clever squirrel, and she knew that sometimes the best reprimand is letting the guilty person punish themselves. That's why she stayed quiet and stared at them all. It was working too. Every single animal on the crew felt like they had done an incredibly stupid thing and would never do anything like it again. It really was a remarkably efficient system.

"Now," Acorn said finally when she thought they all felt appropriately sorry, "I would like you all to go back to the ship. I'll be along in a little while. I've heard the ship is going to be spotless from the cleaning crew I hired, which will make me feel much better to see."

Pounce raised a paw meekly, her tail droopy and still, and spoke in a hoarse, sheepish voice. "Um, Captain? You haven't hired a cleaning crew since we came here..."

"I haven't?" Acorn said dramatically, and then she smiled mischievously, "Well then, I wonder *how* the ship will be so clean when I get back."

The crew all understood and shuffled back to the Golden Acorn, back on duty after their night off. Later that evening, when Acorn returned, every inch of the ship was positively sparkling, and the crew was putting away the last of the mops and towels. Captain Acorn didn't say anything on her way to bed, but she smiled kindly at them as they snapped to attention. In the end, no one ever felt the need to mention the matter of the crew spying ever again.

Chapter Seven
Acorn Goes on a Safari

Captain Acorn thought herself a very well-traveled squirrel, and it was hard to argue with her on that point. She had seen some wonderful places that other animals only ever dreamed of and traveled farther in a single week than most animals do in their entire lives. However, her travel was a little lopsided since being a sea captain meant she had only ever gone to coastal places. This really isn't all that uncommon; most people who have traveled a lot have only been to one kind of place. The sisters in the car once had a stuffed gorilla who was very shocked when he learned there was such a thing as a desert, and another time, a crab was completely flabbergasted to discover there are some places in the world where you can't see water for miles in any direction. It all depends on where you're from.

So when a new port opened to Acorn for the first time, she was eager to go there and was shocked when she arrived. The port was called Savanna Harbor, and it was a coastal gateway to a land filled with all sorts of sights Acorn had never heard of till she looked at the advertisement that had come in the mail. The sweeping grasslands and roaring rivers were unlike anything she'd ever seen before, and she could only imagine how many adventures were waiting for her there.

"Look at this, Pounce!" Acorn said for the hundredth time the day before they arrived, holding the advertisement in front of her first mate's alarmed and twitching nose. "Have you ever seen anything like it?"

"I haven't, Captain," Pounce answered for the hundredth time, and then because she didn't want to leave the conversation hanging, said, "Have you?"

"No! I have not!" Acorn cried, slapping her paw on her desk. It wasn't out of anger but excitement. Acorn was usually calm and collected, but every now and then, something came along that made it impossible for her to hold in her excitement, and this was one of those somethings. "That's just the point of it, Pounce! New adventure! New things to see! New places to explore! It's all so close!"

This just goes to show what a courageous little squirrel Captain Acorn was. Most people, even if they really, truly want to do something, will hesitate just a little bit out of fear but not Acorn. That's not to say that she was never afraid. There were certain things that could frighten Captain Acorn like a scary movie or getting a shot at the doctor's office, but she always did her best to never let them get the best of her. So the idea of doing something new, even if it was a little intimidating, didn't phase Acorn for a second.

When they arrived in Savanna Harbor the next morning, Acorn gave the crew detailed instructions for running errands and looking after the ship before racing down the gangplank with Pounce in hot pursuit. Pounce had more than a little trouble keeping up. While Acorn was only carrying her favorite sword and pistol, Pounce had tried to prepare for everything. She was wearing a backpack stuffed with snacks, guide books, and sunscreen. She had on a large sun hat that kept slipping over her eyes, causing her to bump into things, and was carrying a large map that kept getting yanked out of her paws at the slightest breeze. Pounce was more than a little wary about the whole venture and had even tried to get Bunnerton chosen for the trip, but Acorn had insisted that it was the perfect time for them to spend some Captain-first mate time together.

For her part, Captain Acorn was so excited by all the new sights, sounds and smells, and she was finding it very hard to keep herself dignified. The harbor marketplace was bustling with life, bright colors, and strange, exciting noises. Beautiful trinkets sprang out of every stall as they made their way towards the river bank. Acorn had heard that Savanna Harbor was the most exciting along the river and was trying to get there as fast as possible. After several wrong turns and a little souvenir shopping (which resulted in Pounce buying an even bigger sun hat and Acorn wearing a pith helmet), the two animals found the river and all its bustling activity.

Here, there were fewer stalls selling items and foods, but dozens and dozens of tour guides and adventure rentals. Everywhere you looked, animals were shouting to tourists to come to their stall and enticing visitors for their tours. It seemed the river really was the gateway to excitement in the area.

"Right, Pounce!" Acorn whispered in Pounce's ear. Or at least, as close as she could get to the cat's ear around the sun hat. "We are capable, smart travellers. We do NOT need a guided tour. Let's just rent a boat and spend the rest of the day exploring on our own. Got it?"

"Got it!" The cat responded, taking a bite of apple from her snack bag.

The two animals moved along the river bank looking for a boat rental, but it was slow going. Travellers crowded in on all sides, and Acorn couldn't take more than a few steps without someone pitching their services to her and her having to quickly turn them down.

"Come ziplining in the treetops just an hour from here!"

"No, thank you."

"Explore the underwater world of Savanna Harbor!"

"I've been diving before. Looking for something new."

"Try our backpacking trip! Three days to the summit of a volcano."

"I'm not a fan of volcanoes, thank you."

Acorn had just spotted a personal boat rental stall when a small, wiry meerkat popped in front of her from what seemed like thin air.

"Francois Digger at your service, ma'am!" he chirped happily, "Owner of Digger River Cruises! Spend the day seeing the Savanna in style! All inclusive!"

The idea of seeing a completely new land while still getting to be on a boat was exactly the sort of adventure Acorn was after, so she hesitated for one second too long, and the meerkat rushed on.

"We have some of the best sights in the world in our little country!" The meerkat said proudly, "You come on my tour, and I promise you it will be unlike anything you've ever seen!"

The meerkat was no beginner at enticing animals into touring his country, and he was incredibly good at it. Even a seafaring squirrel, like Captain Acorn, was starting to waver, but she suddenly thought better of the whole thing and shook her head.

"I'm very sorry, Mr. Digger," she said as she turned to go, "I'm afraid we're just not interested in a guided tour of your country. We'd rather explore a few sights for ourselves. Stay close to town. Thank you anyway."

But the meerkat still had a card left to play. "Oh, that's alright, Captain," he said sympathetically and with an understanding sigh, "I hear that all the time. A safari adventure isn't for the fainthearted."

You can imagine the effect that had on Captain Acorn. She spun around and marched back through the crowd to bluster at the meerkat.

"I never said I was afraid of the trip!" She was having a very hard time keeping her voice from getting too loud. "I've never been afraid of any trip! In fact," she leaned in so closely that the meerkat started leaning away uncomfortably, "I *will* go on your safari, so you can tell any animal that ever asks you just how unafraid of adventure the great Captain Acorn really was!"

Poor Mr. Digger was starting to wonder if maybe he had overdone his pitch a little bit, but still, he did have Acorn fully committed to going on a safari now, which had been his hope from the beginning. He gulped nervously in an attempt to regain his composure and tried to face Acorn, but Acorn was already spinning around to address Pounce.

"We'll be taking the safari route!" She announced. Pounce clapped her paws in glee and danced around in place, obviously glad to be going on an organized trip that allowed her to only be a passenger. Ordinarily, Acorn would have scolded Pounce for not maintaining the more dignified professionalism that the Golden Acorn was known for, but she let it slide since she felt rather thrilled herself and figured she could afford to let Pounce have her moment of excitement.

Mr. Digger led them through the busy street to the river bank, where he had a sturdy raft waiting. Pounce, Acorn, and Digger all climbed aboard, and the little meerkat quickly untied the raft and pushed it off from the shore. As they set off up the river, a small crowd of meerkats, gerbils, aardvarks, and other animals stood on the bank, waving and cheering enthusiastically until the raft was out of sight.

From the start of the trip, Acorn felt sure she had been taken in too easily. There was not a hint of danger on the river like the meerkat had suggested, and it was hard for her not to feel irritated that she'd caved in so easily. Still, she was there now, and she wasn't going to let starting out on the wrong foot ruin the entire day for her. And she had to admit, the land sprawling out before her was absolutely beautiful.

If you've ever gone out into the wilderness, truly out into the wilderness, then you know what Acorn saw when she looked around. There wasn't a building or a city sound for miles around them as they cruised up the river, just rolling grasslands and strange trees that Acorn had never seen before sprinkled around the plain. Occasionally, they did pass another animal on the riverbank, and they waved as the little raft went by, speaking in a language Acorn couldn't understand. For the most part, though, the three animals just floated along the river past a world of gently swaying grassland that was so beautiful and constant Acorn almost felt the same sense of belonging she did when she was at sea.

"I have to admit it, Mr. Digger," Acorn sighed happily from where she stood on the edge of the raft, "this trip of yours is well worth the effort. Thank you."

The meerkat beamed with pride, and his little chest swelled so much it looked like he might topple over. Pounce made a noise that sounded very much like agreement, but it was difficult to say since she had her mouth full of snacks and was preoccupied with taking another landscape picture with the camera hanging around her neck. Acorn took in another deep breath and tried to take it all in with a mental picture of her own. After all, not only was she on a safari adventure but a relatively calm one at that. It felt like she was on vacation, which was not a feeling she was used to having.

Unfortunately, as with most calm and peaceful moments in Captain Acorn's world, it didn't last very long. Just as they came to a place where their river and another joined into one, Acorn spotted a strange grayish lump floating near the shore. She held up a paw to squint at it and look closer, but even with her sharp, squirrel eyesight, she had no idea what the strange shape was. Pounce had noticed it too and had come to stand next to her captain and copy her squinting posture.

"What's that over there, Mr. Digger?" Acorn asked as the meerkat walked across the raft to join them in looking.

"It's hard to say for sure from here," he said slowly, standing tall and alert. "But whatever you do…"

If Digger had been about to say, "Don't throw anything at it," he was too late. Pounce had hurled a stick across the stretch of water, and it hit the strange lump with a dull thunk. In a way, you could say that Pounce's stick throwing proved very successful since the moment it hit its mark, the huge lump lifted out of the water and made it clear exactly what it was. The unfortunate thing was that the lump turned out to be the biggest hippopotamus any of the three animals on the raft had ever seen. Even Digger had never seen a hippo that large, which is saying something since he was a local and saw hippos on a regular basis.

The hippopotamus was not exactly happy about the stick throwing, and it wasn't doing a great job expressing its displeasure. Most hippos aren't very good at expressing their emotions, and no one's really been brave enough to try to help them improve. It's not a job that typically ends well. With a deep, rumbling growl, it splashed through the water and snapped its jaws at the shocked animals with a loud crack that made the fur on the back of their necks stand up. Unfortunately, the size of the hippo created a small tidal wave that pushed their boat down the other river. I say unfortunately because they also shot past a very large sign that read: "Furious Falls! Proceed at your own risk!" None of the animals on the raft had wanted to proceed at their own risk, but the hippo had other ideas, and it was the one calling the shots at the moment.

Captain Acorn and Digger were the first to respond. Acorn took charge of the ship, and Digger started rifling through all his supplies on the raft. Pounce, however, had a very different (and unfortunately less helpful) response to the whole situation.

"CAPTAIN!" Pounce wailed in a scared, shaky voice. "We're all gonna die!"

"Pounce," Acorn said with forced calm in her voice, "Unless your yelling is going to help me pilot this raft, I'm going to need you to think of something else to do."

Pounce tried her best to think of something useful to do, but that's a difficult thing when you have an angry hippo chasing you in one direction and in the other is a thundering, menacing waterfall. After a moment of looking back and forth in a panic, Pounce settled for sitting down on the boat and covering her eyes. This actually proved to be the most helpful thing she could have done since she managed to sit down out of the way and was now being quiet enough that Acorn could think clearly.

"Mr. Digger!" She called to the meerkat, still forcing herself to be calm and swallowing the lump in her throat. "We need an alternate course."

Pounce trembled so badly she looked like a sail in a hurricane. It was clear she thought needing an alternate course was oversimplifying the issue and that what they really needed to be doing was going back in time and not taking a river safari in the first place. Terrified as she was, though, she somehow managed to stay quiet and let her captain work.

"Right away, Captain Acorn!" Digger yelled back.

The meerkat was doing much better under all the pressure. This probably had a lot less to do with being braver than Pounce and a lot more to do with the fact that he'd been born and raised in a land where these kinds of dangers were a bit more common. If he were ever to travel to Pounce's childhood home, he would have likely been terrified of things she saw as everyday annoyances. Sometimes, fears are funny like that.

Digger raced back and forth through the crates on the raft, going in and out of sight. Each time he popped straight into view, he was holding something different. One time he came into view with a shovel in his paw, and another time, he was holding a slinky. Neither of these things seemed likely to help in the situation, but Acorn had no choice but to trust the meerkat and hope for the best. Finally, he popped into view, holding a paddle and a long piece of rope with a loop tied at the end.

"All right!" he called out in the same kind of confident voice Acorn always used when she was feeling uneasy. "We need to pick up speed and keep heading downriver! Trust me!"

You may think that Acorn got her famous reputation by sticking to her way and trusting her own instincts no matter what anyone said, but that was hardly the only way she rose to great fame. The truth is, being a great leader is not just about being fearless or knowing everything about anything. You simply can't know everything. So the smarter thing to do is find people you can trust who are experts and let them do their job by believing in them. You'd be amazed at how much a person can do when they know someone believes in them.

That's exactly what Acorn did at that moment. She hadn't known Digger for more than a few hours, but she had watched him closely enough to understand that he was very good at his job and knew this area better than she ever could. So she made a quick decision that I think was the smartest one she could have made at that moment.

"Very well, Mr. Digger," she said in her calmest voice, "we'll do what you say."

The two of them started racing around the little raft, taking turns steering and doing whatever they could to gain speed. Pounce stayed where she was with her eyes squeezed shut and held the edges of her floppy sun hat tightly around her face. All the while, the hippo grew angrier and angrier and continued closing the gap between it and the frantic animals on the raft. It was now so close, Acorn could see straight into its huge, grumpy jaws well enough to notice that it had not used a toothbrush in some time and had more than a few pieces of lettuce nastily stuck in between its teeth.

Around the frightened animals on the raft, the waters of the river slowly grew faster and faster and choppier and choppier. In one of the moments when Acorn was steering, she distinctly saw them race past a sign that said, "Waterfall ahead! Turn back now!" Acorn tried her best to stay calm and kept reminding herself that she needed to trust in Digger, but it was not an easy thing. A waterfall was not exactly a step up from a hippo. It seemed that in running away from danger, they were also heading straight towards it. Pounce opened her eyes to see if things were improving just in time to see the sign and gave another little wail of despair before squeezing her eyes shut again.

Only Digger seemed unconcerned, and that alone was enough for Acorn to still trust him.

"That's it, Captain Acorn!" he yelled back to her. He threw a shovel over Acorn's head with perfect aim and hit the hippo square in the nose, which was enough to slow it down and buy them a little more time. "That's it! Almost there! We'll be out of this mess in no time!"

At that moment, they passed a sign that read, "Proceed at Your Own Peril!!" It was getting harder and harder to believe the determined little meerkat. Acorn was just as determined, however, and she gripped the rudder harder than ever and gave a small snarl that made her feel a little braver inside.

"When I say the word!" Digger shouted, "Turn the raft as hard as you can to the left!" He had to shout at the top of his lungs just to be heard over the roar of the oncoming waterfall and hippo.

"If you say so!" Acorn yelled back with as much confidence as she could muster. The situation was far more nerve-wracking for her since she didn't know what the meerkat was planning. In the same way that it was less scary for Digger than it was for Pounce because he was used to these animals, he was less afraid than Acorn because he knew what was coming next. Or at least, what he hoped would come next. There was no time to explain the entire plan before carrying it out. So Acorn was truly stuck, blindly following along, bravely facing the possibility of being eaten by a cranky hippo without so much as batting an eye.

Their raft sped past another sign. This one had the ominous words, "Last Chance to Turn Back!" painted on it. It quite literally wasn't a good sign, and Acorn took a few deep breaths.

"Wait for it!" Digger yelled back to Acorn, "Wait for it!"

Acorn furrowed her brow and held on tight. The meerkat hadn't led them astray yet and might still have a few tricks in store. Pounce didn't seem to share this sentiment and, even with her eyes closed to how close they were to the waterfall, let out another terrified squeak.

"Wait for it!" Digger yelled one more time. By now, the waterfall was so close the animals aboard the little raft were soaked from all the mist. The water had started to churn more angrily, but that also might have been because of the furious, snapping hippo that was right on their heels. It was all Acorn could do to hold on to the rudder. It was taking every bit of strength she had to keep the raft under control.

"NOW!" Digger cried, and Acorn pulled at the rudder with all her might to turn the raft.

There was a terrifying moment when all the animals on the little raft could just see where the water dropped off the cliffside, and the hippo burst forward with jaws open wide one more time. Pounce, who'd uncovered her eyes when Digger yelled, "now!" was deeply regretting her choice. It looked like rather than getting killed by an angry hippo or plummeting over the edge of a waterfall, they were all going to be killed by an angry hippo *while* they plummeted over the edge of a waterfall, which was the absolute worst outcome Pounce could have imagined.

At the last second, though, Digger threw the rope past the hippo's gaping jaws and managed to hook it over the last warning sign. Now held tight against the waterfall's current, the turning raft shot away from the hippo's angry jaws and right into a narrow offshoot of the river that was hidden in the reeds. All at once, and with a very grumpy roar of confusion, the hippo missed the raft entirely and tipped right over the edge of the waterfall.

Hidden in the calmer waters of the reeds, the animals sat in silence for a moment. Pounce, who looked like she might pass out, could hardly believe their good luck, but Acorn and Digger could. Digger, because he knew the area better than anyone and had known exactly what to do, and Acorn because you don't get to be such a well-renowned squirrel by losing your head in an emergency. You just don't last very long that way.

Even then, all three animals sat in shocked silence, as each one of them contemplated what had just happened. Digger thought about how cool he would sound to the other meerkats when they heard the story. Pounce thought that she would rather face a thousand sea monsters before she ever went on a safari cruise with her captain again. And Acorn herself was thinking of where this particular adventure ranked amongst her most dangerous and wondering if this beat the time she'd had to outrun the incredibly unfriendly locals of Albatross island by cliff diving into the sea below.

After a long moment of shock and quiet thought, Acorn cleared her throat and turned to the meerkat.

"Mr. Digger, that's enough excitement for one day. I think you've proved without any doubt that this land is one of the more exciting ones out there. What do you say we head back towards the harbor?"

The meerkat smiled cheekily at Captain Acorn but nodded respectfully.

"If you say so, Captain. Any sights you would like to see on the way back?"

At the idea of seeing any more of the sights, Pounce's eyes widened in horror and then rolled into the back of her head as she crumpled to the deck in a faint.

"No, no," Acorn laughed as she tried to revive the unfortunate little cat, "I think we've gotten the picture." And they turned the little raft back towards the sea and the familiar.

It was late afternoon when the little raft finally made it back to the harbor. The sun was disappearing over the horizon, but the streets were still alive and busy with activity. Digger offered to show them a shortcut through town and walked them back to the Golden Acorn, where the majority of the waiting crew were looking more than a little anxious.

Acorn had never been late to meet them before since punctuality was one of her most valued traits, so they were all left to wonder what sort of terrible thing must have happened to their captain. To make matters worse, none of them had been really sure what to do if Acorn disappeared, so it was an incredible relief for all of them when the raft drifted into view in the distance with their captain nobly standing at the front. One of the crew members was so awed by how striking she looked; he snapped a picture of her. Later, when he showed it to Acorn, she liked it so much, she sent it to a very fancy painters shop, where it was made into a portrait she hung in her cabin for years.

As Pounce bounded up the gangplank to tell the crew about their most recent adventure, Acorn turned to Digger and warmly shook the meerkat's paw.

"You were right, Mr. Digger," she smiled, "you truly did offer an exceptional tour of your country. I won't forget this particular adventure in a hurry."

Digger grinned back at her and happily returned the handshake.

"I know your work here is important to you," Acorn continued, "but should you ever decide you want to go to sea, I could use a meerkat as intelligent as you."

Digger straightened up taller than he ever had before. The whole thing was made even better by Acorn having made her offer loud enough that all the animals in the surrounding area heard what she said. They all looked at Digger with newfound appreciation as Acorn smiled warmly at him.

"Maybe someday I will," Digger said happily.

Acorn nodded curtly, "Good."

With a wave to the rest of her crew, Acorn strolled aboard the Golden Acorn and the familiar. On deck, the crew was already oohing and ahhing over the whole adventure. Pounce was retelling the story surprisingly well, considering she'd spent most of the action with her eyes shut and her paws over her ears, and Acorn was very pleased with the renewed awe and wonder it was instilling in her crew. As she saw it, it never hurt to remind your fellow animals how fearless you could be.

Still, as the ship slowly made its way out of Savanna Harbor and towards the open sea, Acorn considered all the new things she'd seen that day from strange spices and colors to angry hippos and waterfalls. Looking around her ship, she decided that well rounded in travel or not; the sea was truly the place for her.

Chapter Eight
A Golden Acorn Birthday

It's no surprise that a voyage with Captain Acorn was a long commitment for animals to make. Most of the time, they didn't notice how long they'd been away from home, but there were certain days that were bound to make the less hardy animals feel a little more homesick than usual, especially birthdays.

Acorn had been on many voyages, and she took birthdays almost as seriously as safety on her ship. In her early years as a captain, she had learned the hard way just how more homesick an animal might feel on their birthday. After a few animals had spent their special day in tears, she had decided on a shipwide policy that every animal with a birthday during a voyage would get a birthday party to rival any celebration they might have been missing at home. It was just another reason why Acorn was such a famous captain, not that the parties she threw were fantastic, but that she cared enough about the animals on her crew to throw them a party in the first place.

Acorn was well aware of one that was only a week away: Margaret Bunnerton's. Since Bunnerton was a repeat sailor (and she hadn't had a birthday on the last voyage), Acorn wanted to make sure this was a party that no animal would forget in a hurry. She had plans for everything and had picked up supplies at the last port: streamers, party hats, kazoos, banners, and even those little candy bags that make great party favors. All was in place, and Bunnerton didn't suspect a thing.

There was a problem Acorn hadn't anticipated. Bunnerton was far and away the best baker on the whole ship. As preparations for the party continued,

Acorn interviewed just about every crew member on the ship to see who could bake a cake for Bunnerton, but none had any experience. When she'd asked the last available crew member (a young stork named Featherin, who'd never even so much as heard of baking and screamed in terror when Acorn demonstrated the mixer), Acorn suddenly realized she was the best-equipped animal on the ship to bake the cake. This was unfortunate since Acorn did not at all feel like the best-equipped animal to be making a cake. Standing at the helm of the ship the night before the party, all she could think of was how much she'd rather face another sea monster than bake a cake. Sometimes, the responsibility of being a captain can be difficult to bear.

"Pounce!" she called suddenly, decidedly not avoiding the task ahead of her anymore. The cat bounded to the helm and snapped to attention. "Take the helm... I have some baking to do." And with as much dignity as a seasoned gladiator entering the arena, Acorn went below deck and entered the kitchen.

The Golden Acorn had a very fine kitchen. While I can honestly say Acorn didn't do much cooking or baking herself, she always made sure that it was well-stocked and ready for anything. She even went as far as stocking each crew member's favorite treat in case they ever had a particularly bad day. There were dozens of latched cupboards lining the walls filled with supplies, and the vast counter space had all the latest dining gadgets, not the least of which was the espresso machine. As Acorn looked around the kitchen and assessed her battlefield for the evening, she tried her best to keep her spirits up.

"Right," Acorn said sternly to herself, "if you can face down sea monsters, pirates, and possums, you can bake a cake. How hard can it really be?"

Acorn quickly found out the answer was: "pretty hard." For starters, she couldn't find a cake recipe that sounded like a good birthday cake for Bunnerton. Whenever she'd asked Bunnerton to make a cake, the little rabbit always had just the right one in mind almost immediately, and they were always perfectly suited to the animal receiving it. When Slickfur had had her birthday in the first month of the voyage, Bunnerton had managed to produce a beautiful sea urchin flavored cake shaped and frosted to look like the bay the otter had grown up in. It had been so spectacular; it had made the usually straightforward and jovial otter misty-eyed. Relying on the rabbit for a recipe wasn't an option tonight, however. Acorn had specifically ordered her to stay out of the kitchen, so the cake could be a complete surprise to her.

Acorn had no idea just how many cakes there actually were to choose from in the ship's recipe books. After searching every corner of the ship's galley, she narrowed her options down to three different books: *Bake It Till You Make It*, *Baking for the Practical Bunny*, and *So You Think You Can Bake?* She felt even more overwhelmed when she saw just how many cake recipes were inside each book. Captain Acorn wasn't easily intimidated by very much, but the task of finding a cake recipe was putting up a very good fight.

Inside *Baking for the Practical Bunny*, Acorn found Bunnerton had made all sorts of notes on the different recipes. Some were simple as in, "Goes well with carrot ice cream," and others were more detailed like, "The captain liked this cake well enough, but Pounce spat every bite into her napkin. Only make for the captain." After a great deal of perusing and studying the rabbit's neatly printed notes, Acorn found a carrot cake recipe that Bunnerton had drawn at least ten smiley faces around and decided that recipe was likely her best chance for success.

Now Acorn wasn't completely new to baking, but there is a big difference between knowing how to do something and actually being good at it. There's also something to be said for what you spend all your time paying attention to. Acorn had spent a great deal of time learning how to sail and be the best captain to ever take to the seas. However, she hadn't spent very much time learning how to bake well, so she was forced to rely very heavily on the recipe and Bunnerton's notes.

The first cake attempt was a disaster. Acorn had put salt into the batter instead of sugar and had tried to scoop it back out with her paws (which never works). Something else must have gone wrong in making the batter, too, because that cake came out of the oven still completely liquid and somehow completely burned at the same time.

"Well!" Acorn said enthusiastically to keep the disappointment at bay, "It was the first attempt! I'll just say that one was the test run. Next time, I'll have it perfect!"

But the next cake was arguably worse than the test run cake. Acorn didn't make any mixups in what ingredients needed to go into the mixing bowl, but she did make a mistake about the order in which she needed to add each ingredient. That cake batter had some sort of strange scientific reaction to the order of mixing and became bouncy, sticky, and held together like a rubber ball. It took Acorn half an hour to wrestle the cake batter ball into the cake pan. By the time she managed to throw it in the oven and slam the door shut before the batter could jump out of the pan again, she was borderline frantic. In fact, she was so close to frantic that in her hurry, she completely forgot to set an oven timer. It wasn't until she smelled the burning cake that she realized her horrible mistake.

"No, no, no, no, no," Acorn chanted nervously as she rushed to the oven and threw the door open. Angry black smoke poured out of the oven. "No, no, no, no, no."

She carefully pulled the cake out of the oven, but it was too late to save it. It was burned black, hard as a rock, and had still found a way to jump out of the cake pan.

"Walnuts…" Acorn muttered bitterly under her breath. She tried taking a few deep breaths to calm herself like her mother had taught her long ago when she was just a little squirrel. It helped but only a little. Acorn was still staying positive, but she was beginning to wonder if maybe Bunnerton was the only animal on the ship who was equipped to bake a cake. Maybe she'd been foolish to think she could do it herself. She shook her head a little to push the thought away and got back to work. You don't become a famous sea captain by doubting yourself.

The third cake was the most perplexing of all. By some unexplainable accident, that cake disappeared entirely. Acorn wasn't sure how, but one moment the cake batter had been sitting in the mixing bowl on the counter, and the next, the bowl was completely empty. She never did find out what happened, but I can honestly tell you there were some sleepless nights years later when the mystery of the third cake still came to her mind. In the present, though, she set to work making a fourth cake, but it was getting harder and harder to keep a positive attitude.

To make matters worse, The Golden Acorn had sailed into some choppy seas that afternoon. While Acorn wasn't worried about the angry waves (she didn't consider anything below a small hurricane worth worrying about), it was creating an added level of difficulty that Acorn hadn't anticipated at all.

Every time the ship rocked with a particularly large wave, all of the baking supplies Acorn had placed on the countertops went sliding to one side. For the most part, they stayed on the counter, and there were only a few spills, one of which got an alarming amount of cake batter on Acorn's fluffy caramel tail and made it look small and stringy. It's deeply embarrassing for a squirrel to have a tail that doesn't look fluffy, and Acorn immediately took a break to clean herself up. Even when the bowls and baking supplies didn't fall off the counter, they had still been moved to new locations as they slid around. This was very frustrating for a squirrel, like Acorn, who liked to have everything laid out in the order she was going to need it. A rocking ship is very good at messing up a series of things you've put in order, and the poor squirrel found herself constantly losing track of what step she was on in the baking process.

The rougher the seas got, the more dramatically the baking supplies slid from one end of the kitchen to the other. Pretty soon, Acorn was sprinting back and forth just to keep up with the bowls of frosting and cake batter. She was so busy racing back and forth after her supplies that she forgot yet another cake in the oven and didn't realize it until her nose wrinkled up all on its own from the smell.

Before long, it was one in the morning, and the kitchen was an unrecognizable disaster. Still, Acorn pressed on. No one would be able to say that a silly cake had beat the great Captain Acorn. Not on her watch. By this point, Acorn had her sword out on the table among all the baking supplies. It wasn't because she needed it, but because it made her feel better about how difficult baking a cake was.

"Riiiiiiiiiight," yawned Acorn, stretching both arms over her head and circling them down. "Twelfth time's a charm! I can do thiiiiiiiiiiiiiis." She yawned again and almost face planted into the current batch of cake batter. The only reason she didn't was that the movement bumped her sword on the table, and the clatter snapped her back to wakefulness. She shook her head to clear it and went back to work.

If Acorn had found some simple, easy-to-find trick in her cake making attempts, that would have been just fine, but it also would have taken away from what she was accomplishing. It's easy to work hard when you know you won't have to for very long or that something easier will come along. It's another thing entirely to keep working hard when there's no end in sight, and things aren't getting any easier. Captain Acorn was not the kind of squirrel to give up easily, and, as the hours dragged on, so did her work.

The next morning, Pounce bounded into the kitchen for a single cup of morning espresso. There she found a rather surprising scene. There were enough frosting and batter splatters plastered on the wall to make it look like a full-scale battle had taken place. The bowls, pans, and utensils that Acorn always insisted were kept in their proper place were in complete disarray. In some places, the bowls were stacked five high and were leaning at precarious angles over the countertops. The spoons and spatulas were either bunched together in batter and frosting-soaked piles or in the most unlikely places.

Pounce spotted a spatula wedged in the crack of two ceiling boards. As for Acorn herself, Pounce was entirely baffled to see her captain sleeping soundly, draped over the counter, sword in one paw and frosting covered whisk in the other. Next to her was a beautiful cake, frosted to perfection with little carrots and "Happy Birthday Bunnerton!" in bright orange letters.

"Captain?" Pounce asked cautiously, gently prodding Acorn with a tentative paw. When Acorn didn't so much as move, Pounce cleared her throat uncertainly and tried again a little louder. "Captain??"

"Enemy batter ahead!!" Acorn bellowed, coming awake suddenly and brandishing both her sword and whisk, "To arms!"

Pounce had the good sense to jump back while Acorn looked around wildly.

"Oh!" Acorn said casually when she realized there wasn't actually a battle to fight. "Good morning, Pounce! I was just resting my eyes for a moment after putting the finishing touches on this cake. Not bad, wouldn't you say?"

"Um, Captain?" Pounce asked from where she was still pressed against the wall on the opposite side of the room. "Did you stay up all night?"

Acorn gave a huge, hearty laugh.

"Up all night? No! Don't be ridiculous! I got up early to frost the cake that I made last night. It doesn't take all night to make a birthday cake! Really, Pounce…"

She quickly laughed again to hide an enormous yawn.

"Well, I better get above deck and see to the Golden Acorn! A ship like this can't captain itself!" Acorn bounded up the stairs to the deck before a confused Pounce could ask any more questions.

The day passed quickly and without much trouble. Every animal on the crew did their chores faster than ever before and to perfection in anticipation of the birthday party, all except for Bunnerton, who had been given the day off to relax and enjoy herself as was Acorn's tradition.

HAPPY BIRTHDAY BUNNERTON

Acorn stayed at the helm for the entire day. She quickly found that she had to work just as hard to keep her eyes open as she did to pay attention to the ship. More than once, she realized with a start that she was sending the Golden Acorn in a wild zig-zagging pattern across the sea and had to quickly and quietly correct her course. No one but Pounce noticed that anything was amiss, and she said nothing. She was feeling deeply unnerved by how wide Acorn was keeping her eyes and staring off into space.

By the time the party table was set up in the late evening light and the birthday dinner served, Acorn couldn't remember the last time she'd blinked. She'd kept her eyes wide open all day for fear of blinking and immediately falling asleep. As she saw it, a good captain would never have a lapse in attentiveness just because she'd spent the entire night baking a cake. So it was a squirrel with very bloodshot eyes who sat down at Bunnerton's birthday party.

The Golden Acorn was filled with the happy chatter of the crew and the delighted squeals of Bunnerton as she opened her cards and presents.

"Winter hat with rabbit-sized earholes? I love it!"

"That one's from me and Pounce," Slickfur said excitedly as Bunnerton tried the hat on.

Acorn held her head up on both paws. She couldn't ever remember her head feeling this heavy before.

"A new baking apron? And it has pockets??"

"I got you that," Badgerson rumbled proudly, "I know a badger back on the mainland who makes them."

Acorn slapped her face with both paws as discreetly as she could, but somehow she only felt more tired. The presents went on and on, but finally, they wound down, and every animal at the table started licking their lips and dropping hints about cake.

But first came the birthday toast. Acorn always liked to make a little speech about the birthday animal before they ate the cake, usually praising their skills and hard work and sharing one or two favorite stories of that animal. She moved to stand up with a full glass, but even that motion was exhausting. Her tired legs shook, and she had to give a little cough to suppress a yawn.

"My dear animals," she started slowly, eyes drooping more than they had all day. "Any day we can celebrate a well-deserving animal is a wonderful day, and Bunnerton certainly fits that description."

All the animals turned to look at the blushing Bunnerton's reaction to the kind words, and the shift in attention gave Acorn the opportunity to rub her sleepy eyes with a balled up paw before straightening up again to continue. The yawn was still lurking, and Acorn could feel it trying to find an opportunity to spring out.

"Ever since she joined my crew, Bunnerton has been a key player of the Golden Acorn. She's a hard worker, a kind rabbit, and a good friend to anyone who knows her."

Acorn paused for a long moment. The animals at the table took it as an emotional pause from their captain and felt quite touched. In reality, Acorn only paused to try once more to push the monumental waiting yawn away. It was no good fighting it.

"And, of cooooooooooourse," Acorn said at the same moment the yawn gained the upper hand and burst out. It was such a big yawn that Acorn actually sat back down in her chair to give it her full attention. The crew was caught off guard by this turn of events, and all turned to look at Bunnerton's reaction. The little rabbit was so kind and polite, she kept her face completely neutral as if people gave minute-long yawns in the middle of a birthday toast for her all the time. Satisfied with Bunnerton's response, the crew turned back to their captain to listen to the rest of her toast.

But Acorn had slumped forward on the table, still with her fork in hand and was sound asleep. The crew was rather surprised. It was very unlike Acorn to fall asleep in the company of her crew, especially at a birthday party.

The animals all exchanged surprised, curious glances with each other and then looked to Pounce for what to do.

Pounce got up from her seat, took a blanket from the blanket box on deck, and draped it around her captain's shoulders. Then, with a motion to be quiet, she signaled to the other animals to follow her. They all picked up their plates, napkins, and party hats and moved to the other side of the ship. Hamsterly followed behind, tiptoeing carefully with the beautiful cake.

The party carried on late into the night. It wasn't as loud or rowdy as a usual Golden Acorn birthday party. True, they had all moved to the other side of the ship, where it was unlikely Acorn could hear them, but their captain seemed so in need of sleep they decided not to take any risks. So they all kept their voices low and quiet. Sometimes, though, it's even more fun to try to see how much of a party you can have while not waking someone up. As the crew of the Golden Acorn sipped at their glasses of sparkling cider and nibbled at the delicious cake, they got gigglier and gigglier until most of them had puffed out cheeks from holding their breath and trying not to laugh. They shook with laughter, made wild, silent gestures to tell stories or get points across, and ultimately had an amazing time. Most of them couldn't remember ever having laughed so hard in all their lives.

Late that night, as Bunnerton crept away to bed, still giggling from how much cake she'd eaten, she paused at the door to the kitchen and saw the stacks of dishes, discarded cake attempts, and open recipe books. All at once, she understood her birthday party much better and went to sleep, thinking that she'd never had a better birthday than the one Captain Acorn had thrown for her.

CHAPTER NINE
THE GOLDEN ACORN MAKES A RESCUE

"Come in!" Acorn called in answer to the knock on her cabin door. It was a quiet, sunny afternoon, and Acorn had ordered shipwide freetime in rotating shifts to give the crew a well-deserved break. She'd been extremely proud of their hard work on this voyage. In the months they had been at sea, they'd all impressed her with their willingness to adapt to adventures, and though it didn't fully convey her gratitude, she was more than happy to reward them with a day of free time.

Acorn herself was using a bit of leisure time to examine a particularly old map that had the ruins of an ancient squirrel civilization marked out. Considering the amount of work they had done on this voyage, she couldn't see any reason why they shouldn't plan a trip to the island specifically to see the ruins of Squirrelantia. She'd always wanted to go, but for all her travels, she'd never had the time to. It seemed like the best chance she would ever get, and she didn't want to miss out on such a thrilling opportunity. So when Bunnerton walked in, Acorn was in the process of planning an educational walking tour of the ruins for her crew.

"Captain?"

"What is it, Bunnerton?" Acorn asked without looking up.

Bunnerton snapped to attention and made quick work of her news.

"I was in the lookout, Captain, and I saw something on the horizon." Something in her voice made Acorn straighten up and pay attention. Bunnerton's eyes were wide with concern, and her long ears twitched urgently. "Captain, I think we're approaching a ship in distress."

"What kind of distress? Is it under attack?" Acorn asked calmly but a little eagerly nonetheless. She was already pushing the map away, strapping on her favorite sword, and getting a little excited about the idea of a battle. It had been too long since the last one, and she always enjoyed the thrill of it. There was no reason to question Bunnerton since rabbits have extraordinary eyesight and sometimes can see storms coming from miles away.

"I think it's sinking, Captain."

Acorn suddenly understood why the rabbit seemed so worried. Dropping her sword, Acorn rushed out of the cabin with Bunnerton in hot pursuit. On deck, all of the animals of the Golden Acorn were looking just as worried as Bunnerton, but Acorn was happy to see that all the crew was busily attending their jobs.

"Pounce, may I have my…"

Pounce thrust the spyglass into her paws before she could get the words out, and Acorn felt a little swell of pride for how prepared her crew was. Looking through the glass, Acorn saw the ship Bunnerton had spotted, and her stomach flipped ever so slightly.

The ship was sinking, and fast. Acorn wasn't sure exactly what had caused it, but that was the last thing she was worried about. On the deck, there were animals scurrying around everywhere in panic, and some were just sitting there crying, which is never something you want to see in an emergency. There are a lot of things you can do during an emergency, but crying only helps if the crisis is a worldwide shortage of tears, which I don't think has ever been the case. Most of the time, it just slows things down, so it's best to save tears for after the crisis.

Acorn already knew this, though, so she wasted no time springing into action. Taking the helm, she bellowed urgently to the crew: "All hands on deck! Full speed to that ship! We have a rescue to make!"

The crew, who had already been rushing around the deck, started working twice as fast, and the ship sliced through the ocean at top speed. It was a good thing, too; the sinking ship didn't have a moment to spare. As the Golden Acorn drew near, the distressed ship was tipping precariously into the sea, and several animals were practically running in place as they tried to race up the sloping deck.

This was a moment when you could really see why sailors trained by Captain Acorn were the best in the world and why animals wanted so badly to work for her. Every animal knew exactly what they should be doing and was doing it to perfection. Some animals were casting ropes across to the other animals' eager paws, so they could swing to safety, while others were lowering lifeboats to pick up the animals who had already fallen in the water. A few particularly brave animals, Pounce and Bunnerton included, followed Acorn's lead and swung across themselves to help animals who were unable to swing by rope without any help. Within a few minutes, the sinking ship looked completely abandoned, and the deck of the Golden Acorn was crowded with shaking but relieved animals.

A short, old hedgehog with glasses entirely too big for his little face seemed to be the captain of the other ship. He was waddling from animal to animal as they huddled together on the deck, saying a few comforting words and checking to make sure none of them were hurt. Acorn hurried over to him.

"Is that everyone?" she asked the hedgehog urgently, "Is that everyone from your ship?"

"I- I think so!" Stammered the hedgehog, looking around. He seemed a little dazed and confused himself. Acorn sighed in relief.

"Max!" A small ferret in the crowd called out frantically, "Max! Where are you??"

The ferret ran up to Acorn and clawed at her shoulder in fear. "My little Max! He was right next to me, but I can't find him anywhere! Please, Captain!"

Acorn didn't need to be asked twice. Despite the danger of the moment, she managed to give the terrified mother a comforting pat on the paw before calmly dashing away to the ship's rail to look back at the rapidly sinking ship. Sure enough, there on the sloping deck was a tiny little ferret, looking around in confusion for anyone and finding nobody. I don't know if you've ever found yourself completely alone when you were very small, but the first thing someone usually does in that situation is cry, which is exactly what the little ferret did.

Max was obviously a very young ferret, so it would be unfair to expect him to do anything to help himself in that situation beyond crying. Besides, even if he wasn't crying, there was almost nothing he could actually do to solve the problem of his being left behind on a sinking ship. He was too young to be a good swimmer and not clever enough to devise any kind of plan to get himself to safety using the splintering remains of the ship.

Acorn called for a rope, and while Pounce rushed to grab one for her, Acorn called across the water in a fantastically calm voice: "Hold on, Max! Don't be afraid! I'll be over to get you in two shakes of my tail!"

The tiny ferret squealed in fear and reached out to Acorn. Gripping the rope tightly in her paws, Acorn leapt from the deck of the Golden Acorn and swung through the air towards the sinking ship. The water was almost up to little Max's feet, and he was jumping up and down in fear.

Acorn landed on the deck, and the little ferret jumped into her arms.

"There, there!" She said comfortingly, giving him a little pat on the head, "What do you say we get back over to my ship?"

Max nodded enthusiastically and finally stopped crying. With one paw, she moved the baby ferret to her back, and with the other, she swung the rope around the only mast that was still standing on the sinking ship. Suddenly, every plank of wood still holding together groaned, and the ship tipped heavily to one side. Acorn stumbled and the rope slipped out of her paws.

"Captain!" Pounce hollered from the Golden Acorn, "Look out!"
With a groan, the mast of the ship cracked and fell. Acorn had just enough time to leap out of the way before it came crashing down where she and Max had just

been standing, taking the rope with it. All the animals on the Golden Acorn gasped in horror, and Max's mother clapped a paw over her mouth.

Acorn had successfully dodged the mast, but it did pose a huge problem. She and Max now had no way to swing back to the Golden Acorn. Where another squirrel might have been paralyzed by fear, Captain Acorn didn't hesitate for a second. With Max still clinging to her back, she drew her sword and cut a good sized piece of rope from where it lay under the mast. Quick as lighting, she fastened Max a little tighter onto her back. It wasn't that she didn't think he would remember to hold on to her, but more that she didn't want to take any chances of him losing his grip. A crisis is never a good time to assume everything will go according to plan.

When Max was secure, Acorn raced to the highest point left on the ship, which was pretty high, considering that the ship was now almost standing straight on its end as it sank. Max gave another terrified squeak and clutched even tighter at Acorn's fur. He was trembling so much, Acorn felt like she was back in a massage chair that she'd tried in an electronics store once. She tried to ignore his shaking as she looked down at the choppy blue waters below. The animals on the Golden Acorn realized what she was planning to do all at once, and there was another collective gasp from the ship.

"Hold your breath, Max!" Acorn yelled, and then she leaped into the air and made a perfect dive into the sea below.

Just as she disappeared beneath the surface of the waves, the sinking ship gave one final shudder and what was left above water cracked in two. With a tremendous splash, the remains of the ship sank below the surface, but not before it had sent splinters of razor-sharp wood flying in all directions. The animals on the deck of the Golden Acorn all ducked out of sight as the splinters hit the side of the ship and unfortunately, several of them scuffed the paint job Acorn had ordered at the beginning of the voyage.

The crew of the Golden Acorn was much less concerned with the paint and far more worried about their captain. The sinking ship was now out of sight, but so was Captain Acorn. The longer they went without seeing any movement in the water, the quieter and more worried they became.

I don't know if you've ever had a wait like the animals aboard the Golden Acorn. If you have, you know that the longer you go without anything happening, the worse you feel until you're positive you would be glad to have anything happen, good or bad, so long as something just happened. Several animals were wringing their paws nervously, and a few had buried their faces into their paws. The seconds ticked by. Everyone felt sick from worry, but no one felt worse than Pounce, who was holding absolutely still for once in her life, and Mrs. Ferret, who was crying uncontrollably, as the old hedgehog patted her comfortingly on the back.

"Well!" A brave, familiar voice abruptly called out from behind them, "That's enough life-threatening danger for one day, don't you think?"

The animals all spun around and there, standing on the ship's rail and holding the frightened Max Ferret, was Captain Acorn. She was so wet and soggy, she hardly looked like her usual, well-groomed, proper self, but every animal present had never seen a more noble squirrel. With nimble ease, she jumped onto the deck, and the animals all rushed forward, cheering and whooping with glee.

Pounce and Mrs. Ferret reached her first. Mrs. Ferret had switched her tears of misery for tears of happiness, which are always more enjoyable tears to have. Little Max leaped off Acorn's back and into his mother's arms, where he all but disappeared from view. For her part, Pounce threw all pretense of professionalism to the wind and slammed into Acorn with the tightest hug she'd ever given another animal. Slightly alarmed, Acorn initially thought to tell Pounce to compose herself, but then she felt how much the cat was shaking and decided she could let it all slide this one time.

"How did you make it, Captain?" Slickfur asked eagerly when some of the cheering had died down.

The rest of the animals quickly fell silent, eager to hear the miraculous explanation. Acorn looked around at them all with a sly grin. She truly loved being the center of attention, and this time was no exception. She stood a little taller with her paws firmly planted on her hips as the animals eagerly pressed around her.

"It was simple, really," she said as if she avoided being dragged to the depths of the ocean by a sinking ship every day. "I knew I couldn't pop up out of the water right away since the ship was splintering, and I couldn't risk staying underwater close by, or we both would have been dragged down."

She paused dramatically as the crew and rescued animals looked at her in confusion for what else she could have possibly done. Acorn had to admit it to herself; this was the most fun she'd had with building suspense in a long time.

"So I did the only thing left for me to do... I swam under the Golden Acorn."

The animals all gaped in wonder. It's not that squirrels are terrible swimmers, but the idea of one swimming underneath a ship the size of the Golden Acorn so quickly was both astonishing and awe-inspiring. Even Slickfur, who considered herself to be the best-equipped animal onboard for swimming feats, was astonished and had to admit to herself that she would have never imagined her captain would try something so daring. This story was bound to become a legend among animals all over the world, and Acorn knew it.

Still, rather than bask in all the awe and admiration herself, she did something incredibly kind and thoughtful. Little Max Ferret was still wrapped in his mother's arms so tightly his eyes were bulging, and he looked like he wasn't getting enough air. Even with how tightly his mother was holding him, he was still shaking violently, and his teeth were chattering from fear and cold as he dripped on the deck.

So while Acorn still had the full attention of the animals on deck, she walked over to the ferret family and gave Max a hearty pat on the back.

"But keep in mind!" she boomed in her shrill squirrel voice, "I'm an experienced captain who's used to peril and danger and all manner of bravery! Max here has no captain experience, and yet he was just as brave as I was. He held on tight and kept his head! He showed real grit! I can't say that I've ever met a braver ferret, and if he were a bit older, I'd be honored to have him on my crew."

Just as she'd intended, the other animals all immediately saw the situation from her point of view. They all crowded around Max, shook his paw, clapped him on the back, and otherwise celebrated the little ferret's bravery. Someone even put a large feathered hat on his head. It was too big for him and kept slipping over his eyes, but his ear to ear grin made it clear he didn't mind in the slightest. Mrs. Ferret just cried even harder, torn between still being terrified about what had just happened and being as proud as a mother can be of her son.

Amid the celebration on deck, the Golden Acorn sliced through the waves, leaving the scene of the shipwreck disappearing on the horizon. The rescued animals still felt scared and shaky from what had just happened, but celebrating the bravery of a tiny little ferret is as good a way as any to put a terrifying experience behind you and look to better things.

CHAPTER TEN
ACORN MAKES A DECISION

Normally, Acorn liked to relax a little bit between her adventures. In her mind, it was good for a squirrel's health to get a little perspective on an adventure before starting a new one. Often, she'd escape to her cabin to journal or scrapbook about a particular experience, deciding what she'd done well and what she could have done better. It was all part of her mission to always be a greater and better squirrel, and she took this thinking time very seriously.

Unfortunately, in this particular instance, there was no time to relax and think after the incident with the sinking ship. Being a captain is an incredible responsibility (which is probably why there aren't more captains out there), and Acorn was well-aware of what a great responsibility she had in front of her. While all the animals were celebrating little Max, Acorn's mind was racing (and squirrel minds can race particularly fast), thinking of what needed to be done.

"Pounce! Bunnerton! Redtail!" She called in a brisk voice that meant business, "We have a lot of work to do to care for our new passengers and a ship that still needs to sail."

It just went to show what a good leader Captain Acorn was. The animals all knew their jobs so well, she only needed to say the need, and they knew what to do. Even though she'd been a captain for years, it always made her heart swell with pride to see her crew snap to attention and immediately rush about their assigned jobs.

Pounce took over the direction of the Golden Acorn's sailing while Bunnerton and Redtail started organizing the shipwrecked animals into orderly sections, so they were safely out of the way of all the work happening on deck. The new passengers followed the crew's example and moved just as fast to organize themselves. A few animals even looked over at Acorn with hopeful expectation that she would be pleased with them. This wasn't lost on Acorn, and she gave out several of her signature "pleased nods" to the waiting animals, all of whom looked like they might faint from sheer delight.

Acorn watched as her beloved ship bustled with life and activity. In no time at all, the Golden Acorn was back to its full speed and slicing through the ocean waves. Things were running so smoothly, it might have been any other day aboard her ship if it wasn't for the large crowd of stranded animals huddling together on the deck.

"Mr. Redtail!" Acorn called amid all the noise on deck.

"Yes?" Replied the fox, appearing so suddenly at Captain Acorn's side that the squirrel jumped and clutched at her chest with a paw. Quickly regaining her composure, Acorn continued:

"Mr. Redtail, we will need sleeping arrangements for all our new passengers, and we will need all of their names and other information for the ship's log."

"I already have Wingston, Chipper, and Webfoot hanging hammocks for the new passengers, and I have over half of their names and addresses taken down. I'm working on getting the rest. I should have them all in the next five minutes." Redtail proudly tapped the clipboard in his paw with his pen to emphasize his organization.

Acorn was deeply impressed, but not at all surprised by Redtail's hard work. Foxes are well-known for their impressive intelligence, and Fred Redtail had applied his quick mind to organizational skills and generally being incredibly quick to effective action. Redtail was even smarter than most foxes, which was why he'd stood out so much to Acorn when she hired this crew.

"Mr. Redtail," Acorn said crisply, but with an unmistakable gleam of pride in her eyes, "you are a credit to foxes everywhere."

Redtail nodded politely and darted away with his clipboard to get back to work, though he felt a little dazed from receiving such high praise from his captain. Sometimes, people give compliments just to give a compliment. These people mean well, but you can often tell when they don't really believe in what they're saying. So sometimes, it means a lot more to get a compliment from someone who doesn't give them very often. Compliments from Acorn were precise and rare, and to receive one was a very good indication that the animal in question was, in fact, exactly what she said they were. So Redtail went back to work, feeling practically invincible.

As night fell on the Golden Acorn that night, things seemed to calm down a little. While a little shaken and scared, all the shipwrecked animals seemed to be settling into life aboard the ship without much trouble. Redtail was working double-time to settle everyone into sleeping berths, going above and beyond anything Acorn asked him to do. Most of the time, he was nothing more than a brightly colored blur with a clipboard, racing past her as she made her rounds of the ship.

Captain Acorn was beginning to feel more than a little stressed from the day, which is incredibly understandable if you were planning on having a lei-surely day of sailing and instead, end up rescuing two dozen or so shipwrecked animals and diving off a sinking ship with a baby ferret on your back, all in the course of an hour. She would have liked more than anything to take a long re-laxing bath and let the stress of the day simply melt away. However, most of the time, if you are a particularly responsible person, you'll find that people will keep bringing you problems to solve, and they often come one right on top of the other. Captain Acorn was a highly responsible squirrel, and she knew it, so she wasn't all that surprised when Pounce entered her cabin and said, "Uh…" in an awkward, hesitating way that meant, "I've just thought of something that you need to be responsible for."

"What is it, Pounce?" Acorn said, trying her hardest to keep her voice from sounding as exhausted as she felt.

"Well, it's dinner, Captain," Pounce admitted.

"Dinner?" This was not at all what she'd been expecting to hear, and she raised her eyebrows in question.

"Dinner. Everyone is hungry and ready to eat, but no one is really sure what to make and how much. All the meal plans were set for just our crew, but now we have…" Pounce paused and screwed up her face as she tried to think just how many more animals were on the Golden Acorn. Math had never been one of her strongest skills, and it was showing at this particular moment. "Well, we have a lot more."

Acorn heaved a massive sigh and pinched the bridge of her nose. This actually was a huge problem. Being on a ship meant only having so much food at one time. Everything had been carefully planned for at their last port, but that was before they rescued an entire shipful of animals. If they weren't careful with their new passengers, there wouldn't be enough food to go around. It was a serious situation, indeed. Acorn knew this was a problem that couldn't wait.

"Follow me, Pounce," she said grimly and marched towards the kitchen. On the way, they passed several animals, who looked at her expectantly and didn't even try to hide the fact that their tummies were grumbling loudly, but Acorn stared straight ahead and marched on. She was trying her hardest not to feel nervous. She'd faced a lot of different perils in her day, but no captain wanted to deal with a food crisis.

When she entered the kitchen, however, she was completely taken by surprise at what she saw. All the ship's food was sitting on the floor, sectioned out in neat, tidy piles with a colored piece of paper on top of each one. Redtail was sitting on the floor, too, furiously scribbling away at what looked like a very detailed, color-coded chart with a huge stack of papers clutched along with it.

"What's this?" Acorn asked, stepping into the scene.

Redtail jumped in surprise, and the entire stack of papers flew in the air. He quickly snapped to attention as the papers fluttered to the ground around him. The whole thing looked a little ridiculous, but he managed to stay completely serious as he faced his captain and gave a crisp salute.

"Captain Acorn, Ma'am. It seemed that the new passengers posed a problem with the current food schedule, so I took it upon myself to redo it."

Acorn caught one of the pages in her paw as it drifted through the air and took a closer look at it. Redtail had completely reworked the ship meal plan to allow for the new passengers. The system was so incredibly detailed that Captain Acorn actually felt a tear of pride spring to her eye, and she had to hold the paper in front of her face and make thinking noises like "Mmmhmm" and "I see" to cover her emotions up.

On the other side of the paper, Redtail was waiting eagerly for his captain to say something and was swishing the floor with his long, thick tail in anticipation. Pounce was jumping around, trying to bat the last of the papers out of the air, not helping in the slightest but having the time of her life.

The paper Acorn was holding in front of her nose was full of scribbles and calculations, none of which made sense to Acorn. This wasn't because she was an unintelligent squirrel and more because the harder people think on paper, the more they tend to skip over language that might explain their thinking to anyone else. Foxes are amazing at math, and Redtail was no exception. So while Acorn made a show that she understood the bulk of the paper in front of her, she was still forced to turn to the waiting fox for an explanation.

"So tell me, Mr. Redtail," Acorn said, "Are we in a dangerous food situation?"

Redtail grinned and happily held up another one of the papers he'd gathered off the floor that had a very big, bright green checkmark drawn across it. "I'm happy to report that we're not, Captain!"

Acorn and Pounce both breathed out happy sighs of relief. Her first mate started clapping her paws together and purring with glee. Even Acorn burst out in happy laughter while Redtail grinned even wider.

It seemed that everything would be all right. All the animals aboard her ship were safe, and there was enough food to go around. Now she could go back to her cabin, relax, and finish planning her trip to Squirrelantia. It seemed even better now that there were more animals to go and appreciate the rich history. She could just picture young Max sitting on her shoulders and staring in wonder at the splendor of the ancient squirrel civilization.

"Yes!" Redtail said happily, "As long as we start making for home no later than tomorrow morning, we have just enough food to get us back. No need to worry!"

The image of Max admiring ancient squirrel history while Acorn proudly looked on vanished in an instant, and she shook her head in disbelief at the fox's words. "Tonight??"

"Yes, Captain!" Redtail said happily, not picking up on the distress in Acorn's voice. This might have been because he was trying to scoop up the last of his papers before Pounce left paw prints on every single one. "I ran the numbers twice. I can promise you that everything is correct."

Acorn forced herself to smile at Redtail. "I don't doubt it for a moment. Pounce, give the order to change course immediately. We're turning the Golden Acorn around. Redtail, you've proved yourself to be the most valuable fox on the seas today. You should be very proud."

Redtail was very proud. In fact, he was so proud that he rushed off to tell the rest of the crew what had happened without another word. Pounce was still batting at a single paper, but after a moment longer, she also hurried away to follow orders. Between Redtail rushing off and Pounce at play, Acorn took the opportunity to walk back to her cabin with her shoulders hanging a little lower than they had been just minutes before.

The next morning, she was still in her cabin, elbows on her desk and paws propping up her sad drooping face. Outside her huge window, the sea glided by, but she couldn't help feeling sad about the direction they were sailing. For what must have been the fiftieth time that hour, she heaved a massive, disappointed sigh.

She didn't regret her decision to turn around for a moment. That wasn't the problem. Acorn knew that one of the biggest responsibilities of being a captain was being the one to make difficult decisions. She knew with every fiber of her bushy, caramel tail that she had no choice but to get the shipwrecked animals safely home as soon as possible. Not because she was forced to by the food situation, but because it was the right thing to do for a group of animals that had already been through a lot. Acorn was confident she'd absolutely made the right decision, but if I'm honest, she was definitely wishing she could have made the decision without feeling so disappointed for herself.

Spread out on the desk in front of her were all the plans she'd been making for Squirrelantia, including the tour she'd been working on when Bunnerton had first knocked on her door. Just above her notes, she'd written an excited little "Three more days!" to pass the time. Now Squirrelantia was getting further and further away with each passing minute.

I hope you've never felt as disappointed as Acorn felt that morning. The sisters, unfortunately, knew how she felt from their own experiences and were all too familiar with the sting. In a last-ditch effort to save her morning from being a completely sad mess (which I can tell you is never a good thing for a morning to be), Acorn decided she needed to find a way to cheer up and called in an expert.

"Pounce!" She shouted, knowing the cat wasn't far away. Soon enough, there was the familiar sound of the cat's paws scrabbling over the wooden decks and making large "Whump!" noises when she tripped more than once. Pounce entered the cabin soon after one last "whump!", trying to look dignified and acting like she wasn't out of breath.

"You called, Captain?"

"Yes," Captain Acorn said flatly, forcing herself to take her chin out of her paws. "I need your advice on something."

It's no exaggeration to say Pounce looked absolutely shocked. She'd been called into Captain Acorn's office for a lot of assignments over the years, some of them very odd (she still wasn't sure why Acorn had had her mail a potted cactus to the president of the sea otters that one time), but this was far and away the strangest thing.

"Advice, Captain?" She repeated, more than a little dumbfounded.

"That's correct." It was truly impressive how dignified Acorn was managing to be. It can be hard enough to ask for advice when you're just another animal, but Acorn wasn't just another animal. She was a famous captain and a great leader, and it's much harder to ask for advice when you're those two things, which just goes to show what a difficult job it can sometimes be. Captain Acorn took a deep breath and forced herself to continue.

"I was… Well, I'd been hoping to do something, and now I can't. I'm feeling a little disappointed. Just a little, mind you! I've still got my wits about me, and I'm just as fierce as squirrel as ever! But what would you suggest if you were trying to convince yourself to be happy, even though you're disappointed?"

To Pounce's credit, she didn't look at all surprised or alarmed to hear her captain was feeling anything less than top-notch. She simply scrunched her nose up thoughtfully and twitched her ears for a moment while Acorn waited. All at once, she swished her tail in excitement as she figured out what to say.

"Maybe don't try so hard?" the little cat suggested. "I think you can be both things and manage just fine. Maybe you should take a walk around the deck, Captain. Fresh air always helps me think better. I remember this one time

I was staying with my cousin for the summer, and she wouldn't stop talking and talking and talking, which I always find a little annoying because animals should know when they've been talking too long. I needed to think about what movie we were going to watch that night, so I went for a walk in the woods to get some fresh air, and while I was out, I saw the biggest tree I've ever seen, and when I climbed all the way to the top, I could see the whole forest from up there, and my cousin couldn't even find me because she was always a little afraid of heights and didn't like climbing trees. Which I think is a little weird, because she's a cat just the same as me, and I love it. She always said that she felt sick if she climbed to the top of a tree, though, but if that's the case, then she could always just climb them a little way and not go to the very top. She never listened when I said that, though. She just said that she would feel sick and that she'd never be able to find where to put her paws to get back down."

"You know what?" Acorn said when she could finally get a word in, "a walk is an excellent idea. Thank you, Pounce." With a brisk flick of her tail, Acorn left her cabin, and Pounce looked very pleased with herself for having helped.

On deck, Acorn found her ship bustling with happy, contented life. The crew animals were all attending their various chores, but with smiles and cheerful conversation amongst themselves. Beaverov was whistling a tune from his hometown through his large front teeth as he carefully coiled and stowed some extra rope. Slickfur and Bunnerton were laughing so hard at a joke one of them had just told that they had to pause once or twice as they swabbed the deck to wipe tears from their eyes. Up in the sails, Hamsterly was scurrying back and forth, hard at work, while Badgerson stood on the deck below and called up instructions and encouragements with his large paws cupped around his mouth.

The animals from the shipwreck were out in the sunshine too. Several of them were crowded around a mouse and a rabbit playing checkers with each other in a corner where they wouldn't disturb the working crew. Captain Hedgehogly was sitting on the far side of the deck with an open book in his paws. He was hardly reading it, though, and constantly scanned the group of animals to make sure all was well, still quite the captain even without his ship. Mrs. Ferret was holding Max by the paw and walking laps of the deck to get his pent up energy out. When Max saw Acorn, he raised his free paw and waved so enthusiastically, it was almost a blur.

Everywhere she looked, Acorn saw happy, smiling animals. One set of smiles because the worst of their time at sea was behind them and home was on the horizon, and another set of smiles from the animals who were working hard to get them there.

Pounce had suggested Acorn take a walk to get some perspective, and Acorn had to admit that perspective had been exactly what she needed. She couldn't imagine how any animal could look around at all the grinning and laughter and not know deep inside that making for home was the absolute right thing to do. At least, she knew that for sure now. Suddenly, Squirrelantia, though still a lifelong dream to see, didn't have that same disappointing sting that it had just a few minutes before. It just goes to show you that doing something for someone else will always fill you up much more than doing something just for you.

Acorn made her way to the helm of the ship and took control. With one hand on the helm and the other proudly planted on her hip, she took in a deep, satisfied breath and let it all out. After one last look at the animals on deck, she cast her gaze even farther to the horizon and willed the Golden Acorn to go just a little bit faster. After all, she had some animals to return home.

Chapter Eleven
Acorn Ends Another Adventure

No adventure can last forever. It's the only disappointing thing about them.

The sisters were suddenly warned by their parents that they'd almost arrived, which meant there was nothing left to do but bring another one of Captain Acorn's voyages to a close. None of them ever liked having to end the story, but even the best of adventures have to come to a close eventually, and Acorn was certainly no exception.

It was difficult to say exactly what drew Acorn to the sea in the first place. The oldest sister said it was the chance to prove herself to other animals. The second sister always thought it had something to do with a need to see as much of the world as she could. The third said it was to learn and become a better squirrel through helping others. And the fourth sister thought it was about adventure, pure and simple. In a way, all four sisters were right, but Acorn never really got the chance to showcase all of those reasons at once, except on very rare occasions.

After weeks at sea, land was suddenly on the horizon again. The animals on the deck all whooped and cheered to see buildings coming into view. As they drew into the harbor, they started waving to all the animals waiting on the docks below. Huge crowds always gathered to greet the Golden Acorn wherever she docked, but this time, the crowd was so huge it made all the times before look like only a couple friends had come by to wave halfheartedly. There were so many animals crowding together, the crew could barely ready the gangplank.

Everyone jostled and pushed each other, and, unfortunately, one or two animals came away, rubbing bruised ribs or lumps on their heads.

Of course, the moment the animals aboard the Golden Acorn started disembarking, it became clear why the crowd was so huge. There were wild, happy shouts as each shipwrecked animal found friends and family to hug tight and celebrate a safe return. Animals on the dock who were just there to watch got caught up in all the excitement and started to clap and cheer every time another group of animals was reunited. It was all incredibly touching to watch, and several animals on the crew were wiping tears away from their eyes.

For her part, Acorn had never felt more proud of her ship, her crew, and herself. After all, this was what being a captain was all about. It seemed the four sisters were all right about their favorite squirrel. Acorn counted a voyage a success, not for silly things like money or stuff. She counted a voyage as a success if she made animals pay attention to her bravery, explored new places, discovered new adventures, and helped fellow animals along the way. That was what made a great sea captain in her book.

On the dock below, the news was already spreading about the shipwreck in vivid detail. Sounds of "Ooh!" and Aah!" floated around the crowd of animals, and all attention zeroed in on the survivors who were sharing bits and pieces of the story.

"And then Captain Acorn swung across to get my little boy!" Mrs. Ferret's voice wobbled all over again as she remembered that moment, and she squeezed the already squished Max a little tighter in her arms.

That brought the biggest "Ooh!" of them all, and a few heads turned to look for the famous captain. But she was nowhere to be seen in the crowd or on the deck, and they all turned back to hear the rest of the story.

Pounce also noticed her missing captain and, in a rare stealthy moment, crept back through the crowd onto the ship and went below deck. Her tail flicked back and forth, and she walked with quiet pawsteps all the way to

Acorn's Cabin, where the door was still ajar. She peered in. Acorn was sitting at her desk, carefully unfolding some charts, and a piece of paper Pounce didn't recognize.

"Hey, Captain," Pounce said and was shocked to see Acorn jump in surprise. It caught poor Pounce so off guard her fur instinctively stood on end, and it was a few moments before she could get it to lie flat again. "I'm sorry! I didn't mean to startle you! I just wanted to make sure everything was ok."

"Ok?" Acorn blustered, "Ok? Of course, it's ok! It's more than ok! It's great!"

"Oh, good," Pounce said softly, but her tail still twitched, "If you're really sure."

Acorn gripped the paper a little tighter, the words Squirrelantia were just visible above her paw. She looked at the cat in front of her for a long moment and felt a newfound appreciation for her first mate. Acorn may have loved attention, but deep down, she knew it was all nothing compared to a friend who just wants to make sure you're ok. She smiled.

"You are an amazing first mate and a credit to cats everywhere. You know that, Pounce?" She held up her paw, and it took Pounce longer than I care to mention to realize that Acorn was offering the chance for a high five. When she finally did realize it, she high fived her captain with so much enthusiasm, she started purring uncontrollably, and it was a good five minutes before she could stop.

The two animals crept back up on deck. On the docks below, the crowd of animals was starting to grab their things and make for home, still hugging loved ones close and cheering. Acorn wandered over to the rail and nimbly hopped up, one paw holding a rope for balance, the other firmly planted on her hip. Pounce bounded over and sighed happily as she leaned on the rail.

"Well, Pounce," Acorn grinned down at her loyal first mate as the rest of her crew disembarked, and the last of the crowd melted away, "how soon do you think we can start the next voyage?"

ACKNOWLEDGEMENTS

The more I write the more I understand that it takes a village to raise a book and that my own books are no exception. Captain Acorn wouldn't exist without the help of some incredible people and to miss thanking them would be a tragedy. So kindly indulge me in a moment to thank my village. Thank you...

My wonderful illustrators, editors, proofreaders, formaters, and beta readers. Without you, this book would be a lonely little word document and nothing more.

My family for sticking with me through those rough childhood years of writing till now. That was no small undertaking. My sisters for having imaginations that Acorn could burst from in all her showy glory. My father, business extraordinaire who is always keeping track of the important things a writer inevitably forgets. My mom for believing in me from the get go and giving me the type of confidence a creative needs to survive.

The friends who have come alongside me. Kaela, for taking on the risk of befriending a writer and for not running when I'm in a fit of creativity. You've survived the making of another book! Kendall, for always making the case for some sort of structure and reminding me that I should be writing. And to all my friends who have ever asked me a simple question and have ended up patiently sitting through all my writer ramblings.

My dear LaVoie clan for being the most incredible support system I could ask for. Thank you for always meeting me where I'm at with encouragement, feedback, and challenges to always keep improving.

And The Crown and Thistle, for creating a pub so superb that I feel like all my favorite authors when I sit there, drinking tea and editing up a storm.

ABOUT THE AUTHOR

Avalon Robinson shared her first short story at a student showcase when she was nine and has been hooked on writing ever since. She is the author of Captain Acorn's first book, *The Fantastic Adventures of Captain Acorn*. When she's not writing, she can be found paddle boarding, enjoying a cup of hot chocolate with friends, or planning new travel adventures. She has a degree in history from the University of Idaho and lives in North Idaho. You can find her on Instagram or online at avalonrobinson.com